THE DEMON KING'S
ASSASSIN
EVERERI

CONTENT WARNING

The content in this book may not be suitable for everyone. Please be aware that this book contains the following:

Explicit sex scenes
Rough sex (consensual)
Violence
Death
Mentions of abuse
Occurrences of abuse (not from love interest)

For my besties who love a good red flag and morally grey characters.
This one is for you.

For Kelly and the inspiration you have given me since high school.
You make my writing better, and I'm lucky to have you in my life.
Enjoy your husband!

Chapter 1

Pigeons gathered on the roof of the demon king's estate as I sat perched on the roof of Ethlow, the demon king's estate. I tossed a chunk of bread towards them, and a chorus of coos filled my ears as more birds landed, expecting their nightly meal. I grinned, thinking about how livid the master of the house would be when he discovered the fresh bird poop covering his newly cleaned roof.

The pigeons spoke of the latest news about the estate. Pigeons were incredible gossips, which made them the ideal birds for spying. When sent on a kill, I talked to the birds first. They knew everything about the cities and towns they lived in. According to these pigeons, the pixie was leaving soon, something the residents couldn't stop chattering about all day. No one had left the demon king's estate in decades. For many who sought haven at Ethlow, it was a second chance at a new life, and they never wanted to find out what the rest of the world had in store for them.

I was running out of time.

The shadows of the forest surrounding the demon king's estate grew long as the day ended. Tossing the rest of the bread towards my pigeon army, I stood, digging my bare feet into the cold black

1

tiles covering the roof of the demon king's estate. After months of scoping out the estate, I had become familiar with every crack and hidden pocket of the building.

I flipped off the highest roof, landing on a lower level in a crouch. I had moments to slip past the walls before the magic barrier covered every entrance into the estate, no matter how small. It was best to be inside before that happened. The night had been growing more and more dangerous.

My feet flew over the tiles until I reached the metal pipe that led to the kitchen. In an instant, my body shrank and molded into the shape of a rat. With the smaller size, I slid down the pipe until I landed on a bag of flour that had broken my fall hundreds of times. A sneeze wracked my rodent nose as the powder filled the air. I wiggled my whiskers before moving on.

The voice of the head cook floated nearby. "I can't stop. She's leaving soon, and I want to make sure she's prepared."

"She'll be okay. You can't hide from the pain of her leaving by cooking a thousand muffins."

I poked my head under the door. The orange-haired demon held his mermaid lover in his arms, comforting her as she battled with the thought of her friend leaving the demon king's estate. It was useless getting attached. Everyone left eventually. Or they died. It was inevitable.

While they were distracted, I darted along the edge of the kitchen, moving into the mess hall unseen. The last thing I needed was to get caught in the kitchen again. That had nearly ended with a knife in my belly. If the head chef hadn't protected me, I would've failed my queen. While the mermaid didn't know it, I owed her a life debt, one I never planned on repaying.

The mess hall was mostly empty, except for a handful of residents who showed up to dinner late. No one noticed as I scurried beneath tables until I made it to the hallway. My claws clicked against the marble floor, and with nowhere to hide, I had to move quickly. I shifted forms, growing eight legs and eight eyes. My vision dimmed, which was why I didn't like the form of a spider, but it was only temporary.

With the little hairs at the ends of my legs, I climbed the dark stone walls, settling in the corner between the wall and ceiling. My spider form was the best for going unnoticed, but when a resident did notice me, it caused a ridiculous amount of panic. Those who were afraid of spiders were foolish. It was one of my least harmful forms. I didn't even have venom—not that I hadn't tried to shift into the form of the deadly vampire spider. I found that when I had the form of a venomous creature, my body didn't know how to mimic the venom in the body, only the shape of the creature. It was unfortunate. It would have made some of my assassination jobs as quick as a snake strike.

This was the longest job I had ever been on, and I was getting bored. Queen Math'ara, the demon queen of Valenmae, sent me to Kinzlea for two reasons. The first assignment was to kill the king of Kinzlea. In order for Queen Math'ara to rise as the empress of the mortal realms, she needed the other demon rulers to get out of her way. Demons in power weren't the type to yield willingly, which was where my carefully crafted skills came in handy. First the king of Kinzlea. Then she'd send me after the other demon rulers.

The second task set forth for me was to capture the Shadow Slinger or convince him to switch his loyalty from King Zathrian to her. The shadow demon had once been the most powerful demon in the mortal realm, according to the queen, and she wanted him to serve her. For total domination, she needed the most powerful at her side. After months of observation, I knew the Shadow Slinger would not come willingly. He was the most loyal male I had ever met. The only way to bring him to Valenmae was to capture him—something that required careful planning, because he was too strong and clever to trick into submission.

The queen had delivered a third task more recently. The king of Kinzlea had discovered the location of the Aethrium Stone, an ancient artifact rumored to increase the powers of whomever wore it. She wanted me to steal it before he had the chance to get his hands on it. I could have easily accomplished that task, but I delayed it, letting the king's people do the dirty work of finding the stone for me. Until I completed the other two tasks, there was no point in rushing to steal the artifact. I had time, and I planned to take it.

The three tasks required a careful balance to ensure everything went smoothly. If I killed the demon king before capturing the Shadow Slinger, his defenses would rise. Taking the Aethrium Stone first would raise suspicions. If I killed the king, the Shadow Slinger wouldn't hesitate to destroy me. Everything had to unfold in a tight sequence for my success, which was why I spent months scoping out the demon king's estate and learning every crack in the demon king's defenses.

I had never failed my queen before, and this time was no different.

I crawled up the gold railing that led to the demon king's office. The Aethrium Stone was last seen there, but I hadn't been able to find the exact location. Voices echoed from inside the demon king's office, muffled by a magic barrier. I crawled through the crack of the door, easily slipping past the ward. Magic didn't affect me the same as others—one of the biggest advantages of being a shapeshifter.

I settled in the corner of the room, knowing it was the safest place to observe the meeting below. People rarely looked up.

"We have to use it now." King Jathral—one of the five demon rulers—hit his fist against the desk, his jaw tightening. His black hair was slicked back over two large horns covered in dull spikes. His open shirt revealed his collarbones and the muscles beneath. The demon king of Mithcourt had been spending an abnormal amount of time at his supposed enemy's estate. He acted as if he was uncaring, but the king of Mithcourt was lonely. Anyone paying attention could see that.

"I'm not explaining this again." King Zathrian rubbed his temples. I didn't blame him. The king of Mithcourt also gave me a headache with his constant demands. Sometimes I wanted to shove something in his mouth to get him to stop talking.

"It's getting harder to stop the veil between the mortal realm and the underworld from breaking. If you don't do something soon, it won't be long until we're facing another war. Ethlow is going to get destroyed, along with your precious human." Jathral pinned Zathrian with his eyes, knowing he was going for the heart.

Zathrian clenched his fist, doing an excellent job with containing his anger.

"The Aethrium Stone was created to stop demons—to stop us. If we use it without understanding it, it could do the opposite of what we want. I understand the dangers we face. I am out there fighting the creatures threatening everything I want nearly nightly now. I know exactly what the future holds if we don't do something." King Zathrian dug his black claws into the oak wood, damaging the beautifully crafted furniture.

"I don't understand why he doesn't do anything." King Jathral motioned to the demon standing behind King Zathrian. Master Viridian, the right-hand demon to King Zathrian, the master of the house, and the Shadow Slinger. The powerful demon held many names, and I knew every one of them.

Shadows flickered off Viridian's shoulders as his ire rose. His black tail flicked at the end, just above where it split into two prongs. Despite the obvious irritation, his face was crafted from stone. Since arriving at Ethlow, I hadn't seen the demon smile, let alone laugh. He didn't need to flash his teeth to prove himself. The power that dripped off him was warning enough to the demon king, challenging him. The master of the house never lost his composure, which made me itch to learn what made him crack. Everyone had a breaking point.

Soon.

The pieces were falling into place. With a little push, I'd be ready to pull the trigger. Then, I could return home. It had been close to a year since I last stepped foot in the one space I could call mine. I often spent more time away from home. As the demon queen's personal assassin, I was almost always away on a mission, but this was the longest assignment I had ever been given, and my fingers were burning to get it over with.

I missed my bed and the demon princess—the one friend I had ever made and kept.

"Go home, Jathral," the shadow demon said, his dark tone sending a shiver up my spine.

"You can't tell me what to do."

"Go. Home." The Shadow Slinger's powers flashed, draining the room of oxygen.

Jathral stood, his mouth carved into a hard line. "You can't let this go on much longer, Zathrian." The demon king disappeared in a flash of fire.

The heat licked my tiny body, and I shrank into the wall. I had to wait for the others to clear the room before I went digging for the artifact.

"Why do you let him stay at Ethlow this often?" The master of the house asked dryly. "He has his own kingdom to take care of."

King Zathrian waved his hand, slumping in his chair. His kingly demeanor disappeared, the weight on his shoulders darkening his eyes. There were very few the king showed this side to. If he knew I was spying on them, he would have plastered a brilliant smile onto his face, reflecting the image of a sparkling demon who acted as if nothing bothered him. Beneath the smiles and laughter, Zathrian held the safety of the realm on his shoulders.

"He's lonely and in love. I think it's been good for him."

The master of the house didn't respond. He didn't agree with his king, but he wasn't going to say it out loud. He had carved the perfect appearance for himself, and the demon king missed the subtleties spelling out his true emotions. The shadow demon might have been skilled at maintaining that facade, but it made me wonder what would happen when he finally cracked.

"What are you going to do with the Aethrium Stone, sire?"

Zathrian hooked his hands on his horns and stretched his arms. His leathery wings tucked in tighter. He glanced at his desk drawer. Yes. He unknowingly gave away the location of the ancient artifact. "I haven't decided yet. Maybe I should hold a council with the others and ask them. This is a problem that affects all kingdoms. The other rulers should have a say."

"I highly advise against that, sire. The others only care about themselves. If they discover you found the Aethrium Stone, it will start a war."

Or they might send an assassin to retrieve it and destroy your kingdom.

I mused at the thought. If they knew the irony of their enemy spying on them, ready to start that war, they wouldn't laugh.

"Who says I deserve to wield that kind of power?" Zathrian dropped his arms. He was the least demonic demon I had ever come across. It was disappointing.

"You are the only one who will use the power to protect the realm instead of using it for your own personal gain. Stop worrying about others."

King Zathrian was lucky to have the strict demon at his side. Without the Shadow Slinger's guidance, someone would have taken advantage of the king a long time ago.

"I want to talk to Nyri to see what she thinks." King Zathrian stood.

The master of the house's lip twitched. He didn't approve of the human's guidance, but he said nothing to his king. "As much as I hate to admit it, Jathral is right. You have to make a decision soon, or the decision will be made for you."

"I know." The two words made the air thick. "I will decide, just not tonight. Try to relax for once, Viridian. The world won't fall apart if you take a single night for yourself." King Zathrian disappeared with a gust of wind.

"Doubtful," Viridian said only once his king was gone. He stepped back, shadows swallowing him whole.

I was finally alone. I shifted to my human form, landing on my feet with ease. The desk drawer was locked, but that wasn't an issue. With a flick of my wrists, two thick needles emerged from my dragon scale outfit. Queen Math'ara had my outfit custom ordered the moment she discovered there was a shapeshifter child playing with her own offspring. Dragon scales allowed my clothes to shift with me, so I was never without the protection of the magical material.

With a few twists of my wrists, the needles popped the lock open. The drawer opened with ease, no other wards stopping me from invading the demon king's space. It was an oversight on his part. He trusted the residents of the estate too much and didn't believe anyone could get past his magic and the powerful demon that kept the estate running.

Excitement filled my blood. The king couldn't predict someone like me would be the one to tear him down. I was an enigma in the world, and I hadn't found a challenge I couldn't conquer in the thirty years I had been alive. A demon king wouldn't stop my perfect streak.

Papers and knick-knacks filled the drawer, but there were no signs of the precious stone.

"You didn't think it'd be that easy to undermine the king, did you?"

Shadows crawled over my skin, excitement flushing my body. The Shadow Slinger stood in the corner, shadows flickering around him as danger danced in his teal irises.

"Hello, pretty boy. I was wondering how long it would take for us to finally meet."

Chapter 2

The shadows of the demon crawled across the floor, testing and tasting everything as it went. There was murder in his eyes, and it was absolutely delicious.

The cushions of the demon king's chair formed around my body as I slumped into it. My eyes tracked the master of the house, watching the way his body wound tighter. It wouldn't take much more for him to snap. I placed my feet on the desk, one foot on either side, to take up as much space as possible. It was a power play to show the Shadow Slinger I wasn't afraid of him.

"This chair is surprisingly comfy." The leather arms of the chair were smooth beneath my fingers, and I relished in the low growl that emerged from the shadow demon. Oh, it was going to be a delight to break him. "I could get used to this."

A shadow whipped across the room, slicing through the chair where my head had been a second ago. The Shadow Slinger was fast, but I was faster.

I clicked my tongue, inspecting my nails. They were a disaster, with dirt caked under them and the edges misshapen. I didn't have time to maintain beauty standards. Nor did I care. "What will your sire say when he sees the damage to his chair? I can't believe you would destroy his office."

"Do you think you're clever, shapeshifter?" The Shadow Slinger collected himself, his face made of stone once again. Disappointing.

"Actually, yes. I know I'm clever. I got past your defenses, didn't I?" I smirked, letting my amusement fill my face. The demon was used to the estate's residents cowering in his presence, but he wouldn't get that from me.

"A simple oversight."

His answer was what I had expected. The demon wasn't the type to admit his failures. "Yes, a simple oversight. I wonder if your king would think the same thing. Maybe I should ask." The daggers strapped to my thighs were heavy with anticipation. It had been months since I used them to plunge into the heart of the unsuspecting. I only killed when tasked to do so, and after months of being stuck at Ethlow, I craved blood.

"You've made a grave mistake getting trapped inside the sire's office." The demon held his perfect posture, but his eye twitched. There was a 90 percent chance he was about to attack.

My feet dug into the ground, steadying my body for the impending impact.

The demon slammed his shadows across the room, wrapping them around my neck. My back hit the wall as he squeezed, cutting off half of my air supplies. My feet dangled, and exhilaration filled my veins. This was going to be better than I had imagined.

"Who says I'm trapped?" I didn't fight the shadows, knowing there was little I could do to harm them or the demon without playing cards meant for the final battle.

The demon tilted his head. "Do you take me as a fool?"

"Not at all, but I don't think you're as strong as you think."

His eyes burned into me as his anger bubbled beneath the surface. How far would I have to go to make him boil? "If you knew who you were speaking to, you wouldn't say such absurdities."

"You underestimate me, *Shadow Slinger*. Once we get to know each other, you'll learn what I'm capable of. I look forward to tasting your blood."

The only sign of surprise the demon showed was the twitch of his bat wing shaped horns. He pressed the shadows tighter against my neck, cutting off the ability to speak. "There will be no time to get to know one another, seeing how this is where our paths end. You have caused enough mayhem in this estate."

I smirked as my throat squeezed shut. With a wink, I transformed into a rat, slipping from his grasp. I landed on my feet and scurried across the floor. The demon's shadows retreated from my new form, their fear coating my tongue. I rushed towards the master of the house as a dagger flew my way. His perfect aim missed as chaos took over his calm features.

In an instant, I was in human form again, a dagger in my hand. I lunged for the demon's heart. The Shadow Slinger snatched a dagger from the shadows, blocking my attack a second before I struck.

"This is not where our paths end," I said through gritted teeth. The strength of the demon was impressive, but it wasn't enough. "This is just the beginning, so you better get used to the idea of me, pretty boy."

I twisted my dagger, making his weapon go flying. There was a brief opening to his heart, but it wasn't the time to incapacitate the demon. I shifted into a rat, and the Shadow Slinger jumped back. It was time to retreat before the demon got his wits back. My bones twisted as I squeezed under the door and took off through the hallway.

Only seconds passed before shadows erupted in the estate. They were on my tail, desperate to get me back in their grasp. I turned the corner, and the shadows slammed into the wall I had been next to the moment prior.

There were two choices. Slip past the demon king's magic protecting the estate from the dangers that lurked outside, or hide until morning, avoiding the Shadow Slinger's detection. Most nights, I would have slipped into the darkness, but I had to speak to the pixie before she left the estate. It was risky, but most days were for an assassin.

I shifted into a crow and changed directions. The shadows fell behind, slowing their speed as I out raced the demon. Around another corner, a vampire approached. The dark, curly hair was unique to the healer of the estate. I wasn't ready for her to see me, so I shifted into a spider clinging to the wall. Even if she noticed the little spider scurrying by, she was one of the few that appreciated spiders for what they were.

The shadows detected the vampire resident a moment after, and they slammed to a stop. The vampire paused, her eyes scanning the hallway at the change in the air. The master of the house turned the corner, coming face to face with the healer.

"Miss Satella," the Shadow Slinger said, nodding his head in greeting. The thrill of the chase was nowhere on his face.

"Viridian," Satella greeted in return, not bothering to hide her slight scowl. "What are you doing lurking in the shadows?"

"I could ask the same of you." He lifted his brows in challenge, but the vampire didn't recoil like many others did around the master of the house. I decided then I liked the healer. Anyone who wasn't afraid to challenge an arrogant demon intrigued me.

There wasn't time to wait around to hear the rest of their conversation. The vampire's distraction gave me the perfect opportunity to escape. Other residents passed by on their way to bed or other activities for the night, and not a single one looked up at the insignificant spider crawling along the wall.

As I reached the resident quarters, the Shadow Slinger was nowhere in sight. I had lost him for now, but I avoided the shadows to make sure none of them alerted the master of the house to my location. I counted the doors until I found the one I was looking for.

The room was void of people, but several trunks sat piled by the door. It wouldn't be long until the room was empty, until the next resident of Ethlow showed up, begging the demon king for refuge. King Zathrian was too kind. He let any reject or misfit who needed a haven to stay as long as they followed two major rules: do your part and don't go outside at night. His heart was too big for his own good. It made it the perfect target for my dagger.

If the pigeons were correct, the pixie was set to leave tomorrow. If I got my way, she wouldn't leave for a few weeks. I got my way 95 percent of the time. I settled on the pillow and waited for the resident to return. After a while, giggles echoed down the hallway. The door opened, and a blonde pixie burst through the door with a demon attached to her hips. He picked her up, their lips meeting. I averted my gaze, but in the small room, it was nearly impossible to avoid. It was like there was sex around every corner of the estate.

I scurried up the wall, but a second later, a scream pierced my ears.

"Kill it!" the pixie cried out.

The demon slammed his hand against the wall. He barely missed me, making me tempted to shift into human form and teach the demon a lesson. I didn't feel like dealing with a second demon, so I scurried out of sight.

"It was on my pillow. That's so gross," the pixie whined.

The demon pushed the white stripe in his hair out of his face. It mixed with the rest of his black hair around the two small horns on his head. "Don't worry. I'll protect you from the little spider."

Gross.

A few weeks ago, I was a stowaway on the pirate demon's ship. King Zathrian had hired the pirate captain to retrieve the Aethrium Stone for him. I had thought about swiping the artifact before they got back to Ethlow. It would have made my tasks easier, but I needed the pixie to help me. I helped her, knowing she was the kind to help simply because I asked. The pirate captain was a different story. He didn't trust as easily, so I needed him to stay out of the picture.

The pixie and the pirate slept peacefully, completely unaware of the presence watching over them. Even in her sleep, pixie dust poured off her wings, lighting up the room with a soft glow that chased away the shadows. The shadow demon would find it nearly impossible to detect my presence around the pixie, but part of me wished I had faced the monsters outside instead of lingering in the pixie's room.

I wanted to gouge out my eyes and ears after everything I had witnessed. The pixie liked to smile and giggle, giving off an air of innocence, but she was anything but. She partook in bedroom activities even I hadn't done. I had heard and seen more than I ever wanted to.

I emerged from my hiding spot, shifting from spider form to human. My body was stiff after hours of not moving. A simple stretch loosened my muscles. I pulled at the strings of a leather pouch attached to my belt. The rings inside clinked together as I dug through them, searching for the perfect one. Touching the pixie, I slipped on a silver one with swirls etched into a repetitive pattern. The air stiffened, freezing the rest of the world out. The effect was only temporary, so I used it sparingly, like when I needed to wake a pixie who could wake her partner who would convince her not to trust me.

As my hand pressed against her mouth, she jolted awake, a scream at the tip of her tongue. My hand smothered any possibility for her lungs to work properly. I pressed my pointer finger against my mouth in warning and waited for her to calm down.

"Don't scream, or else." I didn't have to say what the "else" was. Even if I wouldn't hurt the pixie for screaming, it was the threat that mattered. Her eyes bugged, and her fear tasted delicious.

I pulled my hand away, trusting the pixie to follow my instructions.

"Kestria, what in the mortal realm are you doing in my room?" The pixie spoke in hushed whispers. She glanced at the demon pirate passed out next to her. Half his butt was on full display.

My brows rose at the sight. "I see you and Captain Booty have worked things out." The pirate had betrayed the pixie during their little adventure, and I had witnessed it unfolding. To get her to trust me, I attempted to warn her about the betrayal, but she had ignored me and learned the hard way. After the captain's betrayal, I wouldn't have forgiven him as easily as the pixie had, but it was her life.

She pulled a blanket over her lover, but it was futile. I had already seen more of the couple than I ever wanted. "What are you doing here?" the pixie repeated. "If Master Viridian discovered you were here—"

"Why have you kept our interactions a secret?" The master of the house already knew I was at the estate, but I didn't care to pass that information on to her. She liked to talk, and I had calculated there was a 75 percent chance she would have divulged my secrets the moment she was back at the demon king's estate.

The pixie pinched her lips together. She wasn't entirely sure of the answer. "Because you helped me. I felt like I owed you."

I plopped onto the bed, not worried about waking the sleeping figure. As long as the ring was active, the pixie and I were frozen in time. "Excellent, because I need a favor from you."

Chapter 3

The pixie glanced at the pirate. "What kind of favor? I'm set to leave Ethlow tomorrow."

I was more than aware of the pixie's departure. It forced my deadline to move up. "I'm in serious trouble, and there is no one else who can help me." Sympathy was the way to get the pixie on my side.

Her brows furrowed. She knew who I was and why I was at the estate—well, part of the reason. No one but the queen knew I was here to kill King Zathrian, but she had no real reason to trust me. As anticipated, her need to be helpful took over. The pixie couldn't stop herself from wanting to help a poor soul in need, even if their soul was black like mine.

"Trouble?" She breathed the word, fear creeping through her features.

I sat on the bed, crossing my legs. "You know, the demon queen of Valenmae ordered me to retrieve the Aethrium Stone. If I don't return with it soon, she'll kill me for failing her." I paused, letting the depth of my words sink in. The last time I ran into the pixie, I let her keep the Aethrium Stone for her own protection, so my words were meant to inflict guilt.

"She would really kill you for failing her?" The pixie chewed on her lower lip.

"Not every demon ruler is as kind as your king. My kingdom is in trouble, and my queen will save it in whatever way is necessary." It wasn't entirely true, but the pixie wouldn't pick up on that. "She gave me a task, and if I don't succeed, my usefulness will run its course. Queen Math'ara doesn't put up with incompetence, which means my life will be forfeited." That was the truth. If I didn't succeed with the tasks given to me, I could never return to Valenmae or to the one friend I truly cared about.

"You should talk to King Zathrian. He will help you. He will protect you—"

I grabbed her arm, cutting her off. "You don't understand. That would only make everything worse. Queen Math'ara would wage war with King Zathrian for protecting me, and she will kill everyone at Ethlow to take revenge." Also not a lie. "I have two choices. Get the Aethrium Stone and protect King Zathrian and his home, or..." I let my voice trail off. There was only one choice, but the pixie didn't need to know that.

"This is above my head. I can't help you."

I shook my head. "Elcy, you're the only one who can help me. I can't go to King Zathrian. I work for his enemy, and he'll have no choice but to dispose of me. Even if he was kind enough to help me, it'd bring war to Kinzlea, to Ethlow. I can't in good conscience do that. But there is one other way."

The pixie's chest heaved. "I don't understand how I can help you. Do you need my pixie dust?"

I took her hand, looking into her eyes. "There are five rings of protection at Ethlow. I gave them to those who needed them most." She glanced at her side drawer. It had been a little more than a month since I helped her out by giving her one of those rings, so she knew exactly what I was talking about. "Individually, the rings have the power of minor protection spells, but when they come together, they create a fierce magic spell, one that can protect me from a demon queen."

The pixie pushed her hair out of her face. "And what does this have to do with me?"

"I need you to talk to the others I gave the rings to and convince them to help me." I made it sound simple, but it wasn't. Not everyone was as easy to convince as the pixie. Once she brought my dilemma to others, it'd be up to me to step in and push them over the edge. "Oh, and the master of the house cannot find out. As you know, he's not exactly the forgiving type, and he won't be able to look past the fact that I work for an enemy queen. In fact, he'd likely kill me on the spot." Another fact meant to pierce the pixie's heart. "So what do you say? Will you be my savior?"

I smiled, the simplest way to get the pixie's guard down. I wasn't worried, even as the seconds ticked on. If she could forgive and put her trust in a demon pirate who betrayed her, she would trust a desperate assassin who had no one else to save her.

With a heavy sigh, the pixie said, "Okay, I'll help you. Tell me everything you need me to do."

I bit back my smirk. "You are an angel. Now listen closely."

The sun rose without incident. The master of the house failed to find me with Elcy's pixie dust blocking the shadows from sensing me. I'd have to be careful using that trick again. It'd be a matter of time before the Shadow Slinger searched behind the power of the sun for his enemy. I slipped out of the library window, pushing it open before turning into a crow and disappearing into the murder of black birds.

It was easy to blend in with animals when I took their form. The magic of a shapeshifter differed from the typical powers associated with other magic users. Witches, fae, demons, and even pixies had a thrum to their magic that called out to others with powers. It filled the air in an invisible force, unless they knew how to mask their magic. Few did.

But a shapeshifter's magic came from within. It filled my bones, blood, and every cell of my body. It made it nearly impossible to detect. If someone looked close enough, they could sense an otherness, but it was subtle. Without experience, most wouldn't be able to point a finger at what made me "other."

Shapeshifters were rare in the world, so rare that I had never met another. As far as I knew, I was the only one walking through the mortal realm. That was why Queen Math'ara didn't hesitate in snatching me up the moment she saw me playing with Princess Myst'elle, her daughter. I didn't fight it, because it meant I could play with Myst'elle whenever I wasn't in training. I was too young to understand what that meant for my future. If I knew what I knew now, I wasn't sure if I would have run the moment the queen had set her sights on me. Running likely wouldn't have changed my fate.

At least I had Myst'elle as a friend. It was more than I had prior to meeting the princess. The daughter of a demon queen and a shapeshifter trained to be an assassin were a perfect fit. Neither of us had other friends, and she quickly became one of the two beings in the world I cared about.

I was ready to get back to Valenmae to see Myst'elle again. I wanted a night spent in my luxurious bed, telling my friend about all the things I had seen since spying on Ethlow—well, not everything. Queen Math'ara made it clear the specifics of my missions were to never reach the demon princess's ears, but there were plenty of other stories to tell her. I didn't know which one she'd like most: the one about a mermaid falling in love with a simple demon guardsman, or a pixie falling for a vicious demon pirate. My favorite was a vampire and a grim reaper falling in love, but I was biased towards that one.

The grim reaper and I ran into each other after all my kills in her designated areas. She was the first to acknowledge my presence, and it had devolved from there. We weren't friends, but our conversations had extended over the years. It was nice to see her happy.

I was done with Ethlow for a few hours and needed rest. The winter winds guided me to the mountain near the demon king's estate. After a night of staying on high alert, barely daring to blink, exhaustion weighed heavy in my bones. Sleepless nights weren't uncommon for me, but knowing the Shadow Slinger was searching for me kept me awake. It was the first time Viridian caught me in my human form, but it wasn't the first encounter we had had. If he had his suspicions about my presence before, he couldn't deny it now.

It'd make accomplishing my task more difficult, but as I thought about my dagger pressing against his throat, electricity pulsed through my veins. The Shadow Slinger was the first being who held a candle to my own power. The challenge excited me. It would make the moment of success that much more delicious.

By the time I made it to the cave that had become my pseudo home, I was on the verge of crashing. I shifted out of crow form and knew I was running on fumes. Until I replenished my energy with food and sleep, my transformations were limited. My powers came from a well deep within me, and it had its limits. Small animal transformations took less energy, while large creatures took more. Food, sleep, and time replenished that well, and it was rare for me to hit the bottom. Countless hours of training with the queen had deepened the strength of my powers to a level I once thought impossible.

A soft rumble echoed in the cave the moment I stepped into it. I stumbled forward, my legs shaky with exhaustion. A wyvern stepped out from the shadows. His glowing yellow eyes pierced mine, and a shriek echoed in the cave. The creature ran towards me, his head hitting my chest and nearly knocking me over with the force of excitement. His wings wrapped around me, trapping me.

I leaned into his neck, letting my fingers stroke his thick, red scales. "I'm sorry, Jasper. I didn't mean to be gone for that long." It had been days since I returned to the cave with my wyvern.

Jasper's rumble showed his disapproval. He wanted to come with me to the demon king's estate, but I refused to let him. If anything happened to him, I wouldn't have been responsible for the destruction that followed. The wyvern and I had bonded when he was only a baby, and he had been mine ever since. He made the journey to other kingdoms a breeze. While I could shift into a wyvern for the longer journeys, Jasper had a stamina I couldn't compete with.

Wyverns were known for their strength, which was why Queen Math'ara bred them. If the kingdoms ever went to war—like she hoped—she was prepared to destroy the others. If the other four demon rulers knew the dark intent growing inside the demon queen's heart, they didn't let on.

I patted Jasper's neck, pulling back. "I need food and sleep."

My stores held dried meat and stale bread, and I was running low on supplies. It was nothing compared to the food I stole from Ethlow's kitchen. The mermaid in charge of the kitchen had a talent for cooking food—one I had never come across in the five kingdoms. I would have died happy if I ate her food for every meal, but with the master of the house searching for me, swiping breakfast hadn't been worth the risk.

Jasper breathed fire into the pit, warming the cave against the winter chill. Snow covered the mountain above, and it'd take one proper storm to cover Ethlow in that same white powder. I hoped to leave Kinzlea before then and return to the steady ocean-side weather of Valenmae.

Soon.

I would return home to my luxurious bed and the laughter of Princess Myst'elle.

Chapter 4

Elcy told the others to meet her in the library. It wasn't ideal, since the demon king's magic protected it. However, the librarian's magic had morphed it into something outside of the demon king's control. Outside of the estate would have been best, but it also could have raised suspicions. Nothing about the situation was easy.

Involving others in my plan was a risk I hated taking. If there was any other way, I would have taken care of everything alone. Taking down the demon king and capturing his right-hand demon was the most challenging mission Queen Math'ara had given to me. Killing one of the five demon rulers was unheard of. They were the oldest beings walking the mortal realm, since they were the ones responsible for tearing the veil between the mortal realm and the underworld.

They had power beyond what others dreamed of, and they used it to maintain their rule for the past millennium. To kill one of them would be a feat marking the assassin in history. If the queen had merely tasked me with killing King Zathrian, I would have finished months ago, but the queen never made it easy.

The Shadow Slinger was rumored to be more powerful than any of the demon rulers. To capture and not kill him would take magic I could not generate on my own, which led me to carefully pick out residents who had the power to accomplish what I needed to.

The pixie flew to the library where she had asked the others to meet her. In spider form, I followed her. I was relying on her to lay the groundwork for me, and my presence would make that harder.

Elcy was the first to arrive at the meeting place, which was surprising. The librarian had a compulsive need to be on time. The pixie peered between the shelves, looking for the librarian.

"Hello?"

The pixie's call was answered with soft moans. Elcy's face turned red the moment she saw the source. The librarian had her legs wrapped around King Jathral, her skirt hiked above her thighs. The demon king's pants were pulled down, revealing his bare bottom as he thrust into the witch.

"Fuck, don't stop Jathral," the witch moaned, digging her manicured nails into the demon's shoulders. He grunted, thrusting deeper and harder.

I averted my eyes, horrified by the sight. It was as if everyone in the estate had an insatiable hunger. I had never seen so many naked bodies prior to arriving at Ethlow.

Elcy yelped, just as horrified as I was.

"Fuck," Jathral muttered, thrusting into the witch one last time before stilling inside her.

The pixie flew away from the interaction, and I was ten steps ahead of her. A moment later, the librarian walked out from the shelves, a sheen of sweat covering the blush on her cheeks. She pulled at her fingers, looking everywhere but at the pixie.

"Sorry. I wasn't expecting anyone to be early." The librarian averted her gaze, afraid to look the pixie in the eyes.

"I heard you were dating the king of Mithcourt, but I didn't realize..." The pixie's voice fell off. "How did that happen?"

The librarian's eyes widened, making her look more doll-like. She was short and often dressed in black skirts or dresses. Her dark brown curls framed her face. She had an innocence to her, but no one in the demon king's estate was innocent.

"He needed my help, and it just kind of... happened."

The door to the library opened, and relief washed over the pixie and the librarian. The presence of another saved them from continuing the awkward conversation.

Nyri walked into the room. She looked between the two, narrowing her eyes. "You two are early, but I suppose that's not a surprise." She motioned to a table, and the pixie and librarian followed. "What did you want to talk to all of us about, Elcy? I was a little surprised you asked us here. I thought you were leaving today." The human rambled, sensing the awkwardness from the moment before she arrived.

"That's going to be delayed a little, but I think I should wait for the others before explaining." The pixie's conversation with the pirate hadn't gone smoothly, especially without her being able to explain specifics, but big eyes and a simple kiss got the pirate to fold.

I hooked spider thread to the ceiling before sliding down until I was almost as involved as others in the conversation.

"They're late," the librarian said, her lips pressing into a tight line after. "It's their own fault if they miss out."

"Patience, Tareen." The vampire moved on silent feet, joining the sitting group. "I'm not that late."

"Aukina is."

The door burst open, and the mermaid chef rushed through the door. "Sorry. Lunch got out of hand today. I meant to be here earlier."

"It's okay." The pixie smiled. "I guess I should get to it." She looked around, peering past the friends gathered. She was looking for me, but she didn't look up. No one looked up.

"What's wrong?" Nyri asked.

Elcy licked her lips as she dug into her pocket. She pulled out a gold banded ring with a blue gem set on top. She set it on the table, and everyone else went still. "From what I understand, all of you were gifted a similar ring."

Nyri touched her chest where a necklace dipped below her shirt. Aukina stroked her finger over a matching ring with an orange gem on her pointer finger. Satella touched her pocket. Tareen jumped to her feet and scurried away. She returned a moment later and set a ring with a green gem on the table next to Elcy's. The rings flashed in the presence of all six of them.

"What the fuck?" Satella muttered.

"I met someone when I was away," Elcy started, looking down. The secrets she had been keeping made her nervous. "She approached me, asking for my aid. She's been giving us these rings when we needed them most, saying she didn't want to see any of us hurt, but now she's in trouble."

"So she wants the rings back?" Tareen asked.

Not exactly.

"No. She needs each of us to wield a ring to help her stop the demon queen of Valenmae."

Nyri paled. "Stop the demon queen, how?"

"She's under oath, and with our help and these rings, she can gain freedom." Elcy explained things the way I prompted her to, but the others hesitated. Hesitation was fine. I had my ways to convince them. The problem was if they decided to snitch. It'd cause problems for them and me.

"This is above our heads," Nyri said. "Maybe we should ask Zathrian for help if it has to do with one of the demon rulers. Maybe he could talk to the queen and convince her to release you."

My body tightened. I had been afraid of the human having that response. If Elcy didn't talk her down, I'd have to take action.

"No, I promised her we wouldn't go to them. I know King Zathrian would want to help, but this would only cause problems for him. The queen isn't the negotiating type." Elcy twisted her hair around her fingers. "I know it feels wrong, but I trust Kestria. She saved my life, and I want to return the favor."

"Kestria?" Satella repeated, recognition flashing in her eyes. We had met once, but it was brief, and I had been a crow. Unless her girlfriend, Astoria, told her about me, the vampire may not have realized what I was, and Astoria wasn't the type to tell others' secrets.

"Do you know her?" Nyri asked.

Satella shook her head. "The name sounds familiar."

"I don't understand who this person is or why she expects us to help her," Tareen said.

"She said you might say that," Elcy said. I had tried to prepare the pixie as best as possible. She was the easiest to manipulate, and I hoped the others would trust her bright nature more than they would trust an assassin. "I know we have no obligation to help Kestria, but you should have seen the way she pleaded with me. She was forced into a life she didn't want, and she wants to be free. Everyone deserves a chance to be free, don't they?"

It was the perfect line, one I had practiced over and over until it came across as the right level of desperate.

While Queen Math'ara's demon mark covered my back, I had no intention of breaking free from her—not that it was possible. It was the only life I knew, and I had a room filled with luxuries waiting for me back in Aloria, the capital of Valenmae. I had Princess Myst'elle. There was no point in trying to break free from the queen.

"I have to think about this," Tareen said, twisting her hands together. She wasn't directly opposed, which was better than I had anticipated.

"Me, too," Aukina said.

"Are you sure we can't go to Zathrian? I'm sure he would help."

Elcy took the human's hand. "I know, but it's complicated. Zathrian and Queen Math'ara are enemies. I don't think he'd be willing to cross a line that could cause war between the kingdoms. Even if he was, it's not worth the risk to everyone at Ethlow." The pixie turned to the others. "And it's especially important we don't tell Master Viridian about any of this. He'd be less understanding than King Zathrian."

Satella scoffed. "Like I'd tell him anything, anyway. He already has a stick up his ass. I don't need him bothering me more than he already does."

Aukina nodded in agreement. "I think he needs to get laid."

"Who would go there?" Tareen scoffed.

"There is someone for everyone," Nyri said.

I rolled my eyes at the comment. The human was innocent and wrong. There was too much evil in the world, too many beings who destroyed lives for no reason other than a command given by a queen.

There was a part of me that wondered what it'd take for the Shadow Slinger to come undone and let someone past his defenses, but that line of thinking was futile.

"Take some time to think about it, but also think about what these rings have done for you and where you'd be if you hadn't been given them," Elcy said. She slipped her ring back on her finger before assessing the faces of those around her. "Kestria has helped all of us. We owe her."

They agreed to think about it, but it was clear the pixie's words got to them. It was only a matter of time before they agreed to help me.

Time was the problem. It was running out, which meant I had to ensure the dominoes were set up for the grand fall.

Chapter 5

I tossed bits of stolen bread towards the gathering pigeons, biding my time before slinking back inside Ethlow. The pieces of my plan were slowly falling together, but I couldn't act until I found where King Zathrian was holding the Aethrium Stone. I also had to finalize the plan to kill him. The dagger strapped to my thigh burned with power. The blade was crafted from tenisium, a rare metal that zapped a demon of his powers. It was the key to killing the king.

The queen had two tenisium daggers crafted for me prior to giving me this mission, but she had made it clear the daggers were worth more than my life. The metal was rare in the mortal realms, and an ounce of it could buy an entire city. Luck had been on my side when I discovered a cave made of the material on Dragon's Breath Island, but the queen was unaware of the stash I had. My instincts told me I would need a lot more tenisium weapons when I was inevitably sent to kill the other demon rulers, but if the queen had learned of the rare metal in my possession, she'd take it away.

The next piece of bread I ripped from the loaf went directly into my mouth, accompanied by a piece of fine cheese. The mermaid had a way of making the simplest of foods taste decadent.

I wondered if there was a way to convince her to come back to Valenmae with me, but that would never happen unless I let the orange-haired demon who shared her bed join. It wasn't out of the question, but I doubted she'd come without threat. That sounded like too much work.

I spun a thin black ring around my middle finger, feeling it come to life. It was my favorite and most useful magic, since it allowed me to see a second into the future. It was rare magic that many underestimated. A single second wasn't much time, but it had saved my life on more than one occasion. I never took it off.

"I should've known you were the one luring birds to my roof." Shadows slithered against the tiles, invisible to the eyes. They stroked my skin, searching for signs of weakness, but they would find none. Between my dragon scale armor and the magic in my bones, I was unstoppable.

I chucked another crumb at the birds and watched more gather. The hair on the back of my neck stood on end as irritation flared from the demon standing behind me.

"I thought you could use some friends, since you don't seem to have any." I threw two more pieces of bread, but neither one hit the roof. Shadows burst forward, disintegrating the food and scaring the birds away.

I twisted unnaturally as I stood, turning to face the demon. His teal eyes were dark with ire as shadows danced off his shoulders.

"Now, that wasn't nice. What did those birds ever do to you? No wonder you don't have any friends." I wiggled my finger, unable to hold back my smile as the muscle in the demon's jaw feathered.

"And what's your excuse?" He lifted his brow, holding his composure better than I had hoped.

I clicked my tongue, shaking my head. "That's not very nice. If you want, I could be your friend, but I should warn you, I don't settle for boring. I expect at least one dance party and two occurrences of streaking through the woods—for you, not me, obviously."

"Try to distract me all you want, but I'm going to end up on top." His horns fluttered as he spoke.

I licked my lips, taking in his tall figure and broad shoulders. His thick tail swished back and forth, making me wonder what he could do with the extra limb. He was covered in clothes, but I was sure his physique was in perfect condition. "I do enjoy a male who knows how to take control. Well, sometimes. Other times I like to see them squirm."

"You're not the type to give up control."

I pressed my hand against my chest. In five seconds, I'd have a dagger in my hand, blocking the demon's first real attack. I didn't need my ring to predict that. "Not usually, but that's because no one can handle what I have to offer."

A shadow burst from the ground, aimed for my throat, but my tenisium blade blocked the shadows. The demon's magic recoiled from the metal.

"Too slow and too weak. How does that make you feel?" I grinned like a madwoman, watching the demon's face closely, even as shadows pierced the air, ready to tear me apart. I was determined to make the pressure build inside the Shadow Slinger until it was impossible for him to rein in his emotions a second longer.

I bent into a bridge, avoiding his next two attacks. I kicked my feet up, flipping over until I stood straight. I sprinted before he could strike again. "Catch me if you can, pretty boy."

Shadows flickered in front of me, but I shifted into a rat, dashing between his feet as he appeared in a flash. His body tensed, giving me time to fly over the roof. A dagger flew towards me, but he missed. There was something about my rat form that threw him off.

I switched back to human form and jumped from one roof to the next. His shadows were on my heels, but as my feet grazed the lower roof, a hand gripped my throat and slammed me against the wall. The breath fled from my lungs as teal eyes met mine. His shadows crept behind him, waiting for the command to strike.

"Why are you sneaking around the demon king's estate?" He was pissed, and I loved every second of it.

"I've been feeling lonely." I grinned at him, unfazed by the position I was in. It wouldn't take much to slip free, but I wanted to peer into the mind of the Shadow Slinger.

"Don't lie to me." He tightened his grip on my neck.

"Usually males introduce themselves to me before getting this kinky." I licked my lips as excitement flooded my system, but it was impossible to show signs of distress when I didn't feel any.

A low growl rumbled from his chest. Piece by piece, I created cracks in his mask. "I'm not interested in playing games. Tell me why you're here, and I'll make your death quick."

"You're not one of those forty-five second males because you can't keep your excitement tamed long enough to please a woman, are you?" I bit my lip, wondering what was beneath the master of the house's outfit. He wore pristine black clothes with teal ruffles adorning his neck. The demon never had a hair out of place.

"I'm skilled at everything I do." His eyes flickered as he leaned in. "You have five seconds to tell me what I want to know."

"You're sexy when you're threatening me."

"Five."

"I'm not sure if I should be turned on or scared."

"Four."

"I suppose there is a fine line between fear and arousal."

"Three."

"I'm quaking in my boots."

"Two."

I smirked, knowing he wouldn't be able to fulfill his threat. One of the biggest advantages of a shapeshifter's body was the hyperflexibility built into my bones and muscles. It allowed me to get out of almost any situation. Before he got to one, I twisted my arm out of its socket and slammed my elbow down on his arm. His grip released, and I grabbed his shirt, yanking toward me.

My lips slammed into his, and he froze at the contact. The Shadow Slinger smelled like old leather, and he tasted like mountain air. It was refreshing and exhilarating, especially as his brain malfunctioned at the physical contact. Had he ever kissed another?

I had ten seconds before his brain restarted, and I had to take advantage of every second I had.

"I'm looking forward to our next meeting, Shadow Slinger." I took off, running over the roof of the estate, jumping to lower levels until there was nothing but the ground below and the forest beyond.

I leaped up as an explosion of rage and shadows erupted behind me. My body melted into the form of a crow, and I shot into the sky, knowing it'd be impossible to explore Ethlow tonight. Shadows split the air as they darted towards me, dripping with murderous intent. The shadows expanded and threatened to consume the remaining sun.

The magic was no match for me. I twisted with ease, riding the currents of the winds, bringing a fresh storm. The demon king's estate disappeared from sight as I tasted freedom. The Shadow Slinger did not pursue past the grounds of Ethlow.

By the time I made it to my cave, exhaustion was a distant friend. Exhilaration pulsed through my blood as the demon's scent lingered in my nose. I shifted into human form. My hands went to my neck, feeling the bruises left behind by the Shadow Slinger. No one had ever come that close to me before, and my blood thrummed from the challenge. How long had I been unchallenged in the tasks provided by the queen? How long had I been standing at the precipice of greatness with no one close to my level?

For once, there was someone who met my eyes, and we were dancing on a tightrope high above a canyon, waiting to see who would fall first.

Jasper pressed his head into my hand, and I pet him on instinct. "Let's go for a ride," I said, knowing my wyvern grew restless as he waited for me to return. Guilt crept through my veins. Part of me wished I hadn't brought him with me on this mission. If he was back in Valenmae, he'd get proper attention daily, including flights, grooming, and decadent meals. The stable hands would have pampered my baby, instead of leaving him in a cave all day to hide away from the enemies too close for comfort.

Jasper chuffed at the suggestion. His wings flapped, stirring up dirt as he pranced on his two feet.

I chuckled at his excitement, knowing I could never leave him behind, even if he would have been spoiled at home. He was part of my heart, and the thought of being away from him for months at a time crushed my soul.

"Okay, okay. Let me just set my stuff down." I tossed the bag I usually had strapped to my waist to the side. It was made of the same dragon scales as the rest of my outfit, allowing it to disappear into the space between worlds whenever I transformed. It was a rare magic, but Queen Math'ara saw to it that I was provided with the best of everything to ensure my success with whatever task she gave me.

I swung my leg over Jasper and gripped the ridges on his back. He took off into a run before leaping into the air. His wings beat in thunderous waves, propelling us forward. The wind blasted through my cropped red hair. Cold air burned my lungs, and my thoughts of the mission stayed in the cave.

For a moment, I allowed myself to imagine what it'd be like to be free with no one and nothing to tell me where to go, but life wasn't that simple. Before Queen Math'ara owned my soul, I had nothing and no one, forced to steal to feed myself.

But when I was in the air with Jasper, none of that mattered. It was only him and me against the world. I let go of him, squeezing my thighs to stay on my wyvern's back as he flipped through the air. The wind slipped through my fingers, and my body was light as I thought about the way Viridian's lips felt against mine. His shock was almost as delicious as his soft skin, and it made me wonder what it'd be like to touch him elsewhere. Would he freeze? Would he melt into my touch?

Could I make him bend to my will if I shattered his world?

I let go of Jasper and let myself fall through the air. Adrenaline and excitement filled every cell of my body as I thought about what would come next. Before I hit the ground, my own wings sprouted, letting me glide with ease.

Tonight, I would rest. Tomorrow, the real games would begin.

Chapter 6

The demon king's office held no signs of the Aethrium Stone. That was confirmed after a thorough and uninterrupted search. King Zathrian's bedroom was the next logical place to look. If I possessed an ancient and powerful artifact, I'd want to keep it close to me.

Muffled sounds whispered on the other side of the king's door, belonging to the demon king and his lover. The master of the house was absent to my relief. Despite my dripping anticipation for our next encounter, I needed time to locate the artifact without the Shadow Slinger breathing down the back of my neck.

"I don't think I've ever seen him in a mood like this." Zathrian pulled at his shirt, unbuttoning it slowly.

Nyri's eyes shifted to his chest, desire pooling in her pupils. She forced her gaze away, but if I stuck around long enough, I was sure I'd witness more than I was interested in. "He usually acts like he's in a mood."

Zathrian sank onto the bed. "He's good at hiding his emotions, but this is different. Something is bothering him."

The news tugged at my chest. I was getting under the Shadow Slinger's skin, just the way I liked it.

Nyri crawled over the bed. Her fingers dug into the king's shoulders, and his eyes fluttered shut, leaning into the touch of his beloved. "What do you think it is?"

"It could be the Aethrium Stone. He doesn't like that I want to hold a council with the other demon rulers. He thinks they will act selfishly, instead of understanding that this is a problem we need to work together to solve."

The master of the house was right. Queen Math'ara had been searching for the stone as long as the king of Kinzlea—if not longer. When she found out he had a location, she sent me to obtain it first. I hadn't reported back to her about the results. I'd return with the Aethrium Stone in hand before long, and it wouldn't matter that I delayed my task.

"I hate to say it, but I agree with Viridian. You'll do the right thing. You don't need opinions of the other demon rulers weighing you down. They're the ones who forbade you to mark your lover, because they think you can't protect the ones you love." Nyri's hands shook, and she huffed.

Zathrian flipped around and pulled her into his lap. "That's what I'm worried about. I have failed to protect those I love. Maybe that's what has Viridian in a mood. He trusted me enough to dedicate his life to me, and I'm failing him. Maybe he wants to leave."

It was strange seeing the doubts of the demon king. Queen Math'ara never doubted her actions.

"Zath, Viridian respects you more than I've ever seen someone respect anyone. He'd kill anyone who threatened you."

He could try, but he wouldn't succeed.

"You're right. I know that. I'm just... I'm worried I'll make the wrong choice."

"You are brilliant and caring. Whatever you do, I believe in you."

The king's hands moved to his lover's hips, rolling them against his lap. My stomach churned, knowing exactly where that was heading. If I didn't stop it, I'd have to wait to search the king's room, and I wasn't in the mood to wait. I slipped out of the room and shifted into a different body. It took a moment for my muscles to thicken into that of the demon I had been studying for months.

I wiggled my new bat-winged horns and had to resist the urge to giggle. With a cough, I let my features settle into stone.

My knuckles rapped against the door three times. "Sire, there is an urgent matter you must attend to in the greenhouse immediately."

The moans inside stopped.

"Can it wait fifteen minutes? Ow—I mean thirty?"

I rolled my eyes. "No." It was easy to mimic the master of the house. I had spent months studying his intonations and speech patterns.

Two groans spilled out from under the door. "I'll be right there."

Excellent.

I shifted into spider form before slipping back into the room. The demon king pulled on his clothes, taking more time than it took to strip.

"Take me with you," Nyri said. "If there is something wrong with the greenhouse, I want to be there, too."

"If there's any danger—"

Nyri took his hand. "Then you and Master Viridian will be there. It's *my* greenhouse."

The king's features tightened. "Fine, but stay close." The two of them disappeared in a flash of smoke.

I shifted into my human form, unable to hide my crinkled nose. It was disgusting how sweetly in love the two of them were. Love was futile, at least when it came to males. It never lasted. I didn't understand how others could throw themselves into relationships that inevitably ended. It was brave and brutally stupid.

Nyri would learn that soon when my dagger plunged into her beloved's heart.

For a moment, I almost felt bad knowing I would be the one to destroy their dreams.

Almost.

My bag of rings jingled as I pulled them from my pocket. I searched for the one that would warn me thirty seconds before anyone approached in a ten meter radius. It wasn't much time, but it was enough to shrink to a creature that was overlooked. There was limited time before the demon king would return, confused when his second in command was nowhere to be found, and there were no issues with the greenhouse.

Five minutes at most.

If I was unlucky, he'd be back sooner.

If I was really unlucky, the Shadow Slinger would be in tow. The moment the king went to Viridian to clarify his confusion, the master of the house would know what had happened. He was too smart to be confused.

The dressers were void of artifacts. The closet had nothing of significance—except for some straps that drew my attention. I tucked the information away for later. Under the bed was empty. Even the locked trunk—the lock was infant-level easy to pick—had various powerful items, but none of them held the Aethrium Stone. I pocketed a handful of coins—the king wouldn't miss them—before locking the door.

The king's room was another failure, and I was out of time. I pushed open the window before turning into a crow and diving into the cold air.

Chapter 7

I circled above Ethlow, using the cover of night to hide my presence. It wasn't the Shadow Slinger that threatened me without the sun's protection. Outside the estate, cracks between the veil separating the underworld and the mortal realm formed, releasing dark creatures that had been twisted in death.

Cracks began forming in the kingdoms near the demon rulers. At first, it was manageable. Queen Math'ara easily sealed the first crack that appeared in Valenmae, but with time, more and more formed beneath her castle. She sent me to investigate other kingdoms. It didn't take much to learn the other demon rulers were facing the same issue.

The ruler of the underworld was trying to destroy the veil separating the worlds. According to Math'ara, it was because he couldn't stand knowing that the demon rulers of the mortal realms bested him in the Great Demon War a millennium ago. It was the word of a demon, which meant there was more to the story than that. I had thought about looking for the truth, but it wasn't my job to sort through the lies of Queen Math'ara. It was my job to complete the tasks set forth for me.

Something I couldn't do without locating the Aethrium Stone.

Or if the others refused to help.

I swooped down, aiming for a window I had peered into a handful of times. Coming and going in the estate was easy after sunset, but windows were the easiest to slip through, especially if I got a resident to open it for me. I clicked my beak against the glass incessantly. The healer wouldn't be able to ignore my presence if I made the sound as obnoxious as possible.

After a moment, the window slid open.

"What the fuck?"

I flew into the room, and a scream pierced my ears. I landed on the table across the room and hopped to face the vampire. Her hands were over her head as she crouched on the ground, frozen in fear.

"What's wrong?" A flash of pink and purple ombre hair appeared suddenly. The power of the underworld filled the room, but it differed from the creatures outside. It was contained and molded into an unyielding power.

The grim reaper glanced at me and then back at the vampire. Laughter took over her entire body as she clutched her waist. "Are you scared of the bird?" She leaned over and ruffled the vampire's hair before closing the window.

"What are you doing? You have to get it out of here." The vampire's eyes were wide as she looked at me.

"Careful, she won't like that." The grim reaper smirked knowingly.

"What are you talking about?"

In a flash, I switched to my human form, sitting on the desk. I flicked my hands as I said, "Boo."

Another delicious scream rang in my ears.

The grim reaper rushed over and enveloped me in a hug. My body tensed, but she ignored it. "It's been so long since I've seen you."

I patted her on the back a few times. "It's only been a few months."

"Yeah, but you stayed in crow form, which makes it hard to hug you." It was the exact reason I had stayed in crow form when I approached her last time.

A throat cleared from the corner of the room. "Astoria, you know this... crow?"

The grim reaper dragged me over to the vampire. "Satella, meet Kestria. Kestria, meet Satella. You have technically met before, but you need a proper introduction."

I pulled away and circled the vampire, looking her up and down. "So, you're the one who stole the grim reaper's heart. Interesting."

"And you're the one who convinced Elcy to help you." The vampire held her chin high, despite her initial reaction to my presence.

"You don't like me, do you?"

The vampire shifted in place. I made her nervous, but she wasn't the type to admit it. "I don't know you, and you're asking us to do something dangerous."

"If getting to know me is the problem, we can fix that." I poked the vampire's nose before flipping on my heels. I burst into the side room connected to the infirmary and looked around. The vampire lived near the infirmary, so if anyone needed treatment, she was ready. It was rare for serious injuries to take place at the estate, but recent months had changed that. The mortal realm was growing dangerous with the threat of the underworld looming, but few beyond the demon rulers knew the extent of the peril the world would face if someone didn't fix it soon.

The vampire's bed was made with excess blankets and pillows. She liked comfort, despite not needing to sleep. Several glass tanks lined her desks, filled with bugs. A black tarantula pulled my attention first. I reached into the tank without hesitation, and the eight-legged creature climbed onto my hand.

"What are you doing? This is my room!" The vampire stormed in after me.

Astoria appeared above the bed, hovering in the air upside down. "We could have a slumber party!"

"I call the bed!" It had been months since I slept on a proper mattress—not that I would've been able to relax enough to sleep knowing the Shadow Slinger could detect my presence at any second.

"I have not agreed to this." The vampire crossed her arms and huffed. Her reaction only made it more fun.

I set the tarantula down before turning back to Satella. "You don't want to help me, because you don't know if you can trust me. So, ask me anything you want. I'm an open book."

Satella took a slow breath, looking between Astoria and me. If she wanted her girlfriend's approval, she would get it—not that

Astoria was the best source to rely on. I could tell the grim reaper I was going to kill a saint, and she'd wish me luck. Grim reapers were born to be neutral, which was why finding out she was in love had been a shock.

"Give me one good reason why I should help you while keeping a potential threat a secret from the demon king who gave me sanctuary." The vampire placed her hands on her hips and watched me expectantly.

I walked past her and jumped on the bed, stretching my limbs as my body sank onto the soft, feather-stuffed mattress. "I could get used to this."

"Are you going to ignore me?"

"Her bed is the best." Astoria plopped on the mattress next to me. "It's a shame I'm so busy these days and can't sleep over more."

"Reapers don't sleep," I pointed out.

"No, but there are plenty of other things we do in this bed." Her wink made me painfully aware of where I was.

I sat up slowly, cringing. "Maybe I don't want the bed."

"We're not having a sleepover, so it doesn't matter." Satella grabbed my hand, but I resisted, easily pulling her onto the mattress with the reaper and me.

"I didn't expect to have a threesome when I came here, but if that convinces you to help me, I would consider it." An evil grin painted my lips as I looked the vampire directly in the eyes.

Satella was on her feet a second later. "If you want me to help you, this isn't the way to do it. I'm done." She pursed her lips, but she was only trying to hide her amusement. If she was with someone like Astoria, then she didn't mind my antics.

Astoria disappeared, reappearing behind the vampire. The reaper wrapped her arms around her girlfriend, resting her chin on the vampire's shoulder. "Give her a chance. For me?" She pressed a kiss against the vampire's neck.

Satella sighed, dramatically rolling her eyes. "You have two minutes."

I grinned, knowing this was going to be a breeze. I had watched the healer long enough to understand the way to her heart. "Because this isn't the life I wanted."

"I don't understand."

I took a slow breath, gathering the most sympathetic memories of my life. "I was only five years old when Queen Math'ara took me in and gave me this." I lifted my shirt, turning to show the mark that covered nearly my entire back. A vine with thorns weaved over my spine until it blossomed into a bleeding rose that spread over my shoulder blades. It was impossible to see without standing in front of a mirror, but I felt each line burned into my skin.

Satella gasped, placing a hand over her mouth. "Is that..." Her voice fell off, as if she couldn't understand what the design on my back was.

"The mark of a demon queen? Why, yes, it is. It has been there since Queen Math'ara roped me into her service as a child. If I don't do as she says, the mark on my back will kill me, which is where you and those rings come in handy. If the five of you agree to help me,

I can trap Queen Math'ara before she kills me and free myself from her chains."

The vampire's eyes glistened, but she wasn't fully convinced. "Why do you deserve freedom? You're an assassin, which means you've killed countless people, right?"

They weren't countless deaths. I remembered every one. I held the vampire's gaze, wanting her to feel my words. "So have you. Don't we all deserve a second chance at a new life, one we weren't forced into?" After months of stalking the estate, I knew about Satella's past. When she was first turned into a vampire, she had gone through a killing spree, unable to satiate her blood lust. She hated herself and her life, which was how she ended up at Ethlow. It was her second chance, which was how I knew my words sliced her clean open.

Satella's shoulders fell. "Okay."

"Okay?"

The vampire rolled her eyes again. "You want a second chance? I'll help you get one."

"Does that mean she can stay tonight?" Astoria jumped on the bed, earning a glare from the vampire.

"I guess." Satella acted like she wasn't thrilled.

"Who's stealing snacks from the kitchen?" I asked.

"On it!" The grim reaper disappeared in a flash. I had never spent more than a few moments with the reaper after she came to collect the soul of the being I had killed, but it'd be nice to get to know her better. With our line of work, we were bound to see each other again.

"Don't make me regret this," Satella said the moment it was just the two of us.

I didn't respond, not interested in lying to her again. She would regret helping me. All of them would, but it was either me or them, and I had to put myself first. It was the only way to survive.

Chapter 8

I walked along the peak of the roof, practicing my perfect balance. The roof slanted on either side of me, adding to the charm of the estate. It was different from the flat roofs of Valenmae. It made it fun to play, and I had to have as much fun as possible before returning to the queen. She wasn't going to be happy with how long I took. She rarely was.

Satella and Elcy were on my side. It was a matter of getting the other three to help while keeping it a secret. I had to walk a careful line with them. The demon king's lover had a soft heart. A good sob story should convince her. The only problem was ensuring she kept the secret from the demon king. Her love for him ran deep, which made it difficult to imagine her keeping my request from him. There was a 60 percent chance the king already knew about me.

Every day I wasted searching for the Aethrium Stone and convincing the others put the mission in danger. My heart thumped against my chest, reminding me of the risks hanging over my head. I didn't like working with others. They were too unpredictable.

I sank into a crouch and eyed the roof of the greenhouse peeking through the forest. The demon king's lover spent most of her time there. It was a short walk from the estate and away from the eyes of the king and his second in command. It was the perfect place to talk to her. That'd have to wait, though.

Shadows crawled over the roof of the tile, feeling for my presence. Most would have run from the slithering power, but I wasn't afraid.

"Does that trick normally work to scare residents away?" The sun hung high in the sky, giving less places for the demon's shadows to hide. He was getting brazen if he was willing to come after me when anyone could look up and see the two of us.

I slipped a ring on my finger, keeping the movement practically nonexistent.

"Sometimes." The demon's voice brushed my ear.

"Did you think it'd work on me?" I counted the seconds of conversation I had before things turned bloody.

"I haven't figured out what scares you yet." To the untrained ear, the ire building inside the demon would have been silent. He liked to be in control, which meant understanding everyone around him. The slight hitch in his voice gave me all the information I needed.

"Keep searching, but you'll never figure it out." I straightened my legs, digging my toes into the wood beneath my feet.

"Everyone is afraid of something."

I flipped around, but the Shadow Slinger wasn't there. "What are you afraid of?" There was a .001 percent chance he would admit the truth. His king didn't know the answer. He knew the

Master of the House better than most, but there were secrets the shadow demon kept hidden. It reminded me of myself.

"I'd tell you, but you won't be around long enough for it to matter." His fingers brushed over my side, but when I turned around, he was gone again.

The Shadow Slinger was playing games.

A smirk tugged at my features. "You're the type to play hard to get, aren't you? It works well, but at some point you have to stop running, or you'll end up alone."

"And what about you?" His breath brushed against my ear, but this time I didn't bother to move. He wasn't standing behind me. He was a ghost in the wind.

"Trying to get to know me? I'm shocked. Maybe you'll make a friend after all, pretty boy." I licked my lips, biding my time. I had anticipated the Shadow Slinger to attack twenty seconds ago, but my calculations were wrong. A rare thing to happen.

"I already know everything I need to know about you, Kestria."

I picked at my nails, acting as if my name on his tongue hadn't done something to my spine. "You know my name. I'm impressed, pretty boy, or should I say Viridian, since we're showing off useless information?"

The shadows hiding under the small space between tiles shrank as the air turned acrid. Viridian appeared several feet in front of me, holding two daggers. "You are Queen Math'ara's personal assassin. You have caused trouble across the five kingdoms, yet many don't know who or what you are. Those who do know you call you the

Infernal Dagger, because you strike with precision and are gone in a flash."

My hand hovered over a simple silver dagger. My tenisium dagger wasn't necessary for this fight. It was meant for the demon king. "You've done your research. I'm impressed. What else?" I waited for him to say he knew exactly why I was at Ethlow before unleashing his full fury on me. If Nyri had told her beloved about my request, the demon king would have gone straight to his most loyal companion. The king would have done so out of kindness, but the master of the house would have known instantly it was a farce.

"There are no records of you before you turned five, which means Queen Math'ara erased your history, or she doesn't know what happened to you before you showed up and started playing with her daughter. You are friends with the demon princess of Valenmae, and you have a pet wyvern."

I twisted my dagger to reflect the sun into the demon's eyes. "I'm impressed." And I was. "No one has discerned that much information about me before." It was a little unnerving. The thought of the Shadow Slinger using the two beings I cared about against me chilled my blood. I didn't know if he'd stoop to that kind of level, but I didn't doubt how low a demon could go.

"There is one thing I haven't been able to learn."

I quirked my eyebrows, wishing I could lift only one for a more dramatic effect. "Let me guess. That bit of information is why you haven't attacked me yet?"

I knew what words were going to come out of the Shadow Slinger's mouth before they hit my ears. "Why is Queen Math'ara's assassin hanging around Ethlow?"

I couldn't stop the cackle that slipped past my lips. If Viridian knew why I was at Ethlow, he wouldn't have hesitated to attempt to slit my throat, but he didn't know. Nyri hadn't spilled my secret. "You'll have to kill me if you want that information. Oh, wait."

My laugh triggered something within the demon. He disappeared, reappearing behind me, but I was already on the run. His shadows snapped at my heels as I dashed and twisted out of the way. He was furious, and I was elated, unable to stop the giggle that spilled each time he missed.

I jumped, diving for the lower level of the roof. Viridian appeared where I was about to land, so I shifted into crow form. Two wing flaps sent me flying, but shadows wrapped around my leg, ripping me out of the air. I was in human form when my back hit the roof. Bruises pelted my body as I rolled from the impact. I stabbed my dagger into the tiles, cracking a tile as I halted.

The Shadow Slinger didn't give me a moment to breathe. He was on me a moment later. I saw his attack coming, but I was too slow. His shadows hit the dagger out of my hand, sending it scattering off the roof. He pressed his hips between my legs to restrict my movement. He pinned my hands with his while his shadows stopped us from sliding down the steep roof. The demon's teal eyes darkened as he squeezed my wrists hard enough to snap the bones of someone with less agility.

"Why did Queen Math'ara send you here?" His voice was flat, but his eyes gave away the emotions burning inside. Cracks destroyed his perfect mask, and if I pushed a little harder, his facade would shatter.

"Normally, someone has to buy me a few meals before getting me into this position." I shifted, testing my range of motion. It wasn't much with the weight of the demon pressing down on me. A simple shift would have freed me, but I wanted to play a little longer.

A low growl escaped the demon's lips as his horns fluttered. He pressed his hips harder against mine, creating palpable friction between us. "If Queen Math'ara has sent you here to hurt King Zathrian, it will cause a war. Do you understand what that would mean for many innocent lives, shapeshifter?"

I knew exactly what war entailed. While there hadn't been a major war since the Great Demon Wars that happened a millennium ago, I had been sent to take out generals of small factions that attempted to rise against my demon queen.

"I'm not interested in starting a war," I said, my features cooling.

"I will give you one last chance to answer me."

"Tell me this, Shadow Slinger. If you are so concerned about why I'm here, why haven't you told your precious king about my presence yet?" The question had been bubbling in the back of my head since our first interaction. Viridian was a slave to the king, yet he acted as if he was the one in charge. I didn't understand the dynamic between the two of them.

"Because the sire doesn't need to know about every pesky nuisance that appears within the estate. He has more important things to worry about."

"Like how he is going to protect his precious kingdom from the underworld?" I studied the demon's face, delighted by the provoked response. "Your king is not the only one facing struggles. I am here to learn how to protect my kingdom—to protect those I love. I'd say the same as you, but I'm not convinced you love anyone in this world."

Viridian's chest rumbled as his form shifted to resemble a proper demon. Claws pierced my wrists, making blood drip onto the roof. The tips of his tail sharpened into razor points as he aimed it towards my throat. His skin darkened to the color of ash as his mouth filled with sharp teeth that could shred skin with ease. I had enough of the compromising position, and I shifted into rat form, knowing what it did to the master of the house. He jumped back as I scurried free, but I had to dodge several daggers as I bolted over the black tiles. I flew off the edge of the roof, switching into human form as I flipped to the ground. The moment my feet touched the dirt, a hand was in my hair. He had moved faster than my ring could predict.

The Shadow Slinger slammed my head against the brick wall, making my ears ring.

"You must have a death wish," he said lowly. "If you won't tell me why you're here, then I have no choice but to kill you."

"And what will you do when Queen Math'ara shows up at your sire's doorstep, demanding retribution? Killing me will ruin the delicate peace between kingdoms."

My words gave the Shadow Slinger pause, opening up an opportunity for me. I grabbed his wrist and spun our bodies around. I slammed his face against the wall, and the smell of iron hit my nose. I shifted into a falcon, darting into the sky before disappearing in the blink of an eye.

My body ripped through space. My legs shook as the effect of the magic ring wore off. I stumbled into the cave, knowing I was safe from the eyes of the demon this far away from Ethlow. I tossed my ring into the bag, the teleportation magic drained. My head thrummed from the force of it hitting the brick wall. Jasper rushed up to me. He nuzzled my chest, and I pet him involuntarily.

I laughed as my fingers touched my forehead. Blood coated my hand, which made Jasper whimper. I licked my lips at the sight. It had been a long time since someone made me bleed. It was invigorating, and I couldn't wait to return the favor.

Chapter 9

Gray clouds hung low in the sky. They weren't dark enough for rain. They were the type that hid away the sun and made winter shout at the world. I flew above the forest, keeping a close eye on the two horses below as they made their way to the lake closest to the demon king's estate. It was too cold for a swim in the water, but that didn't matter to a mermaid who grew up in the frigid ocean.

The orange-haired demon acted like a beacon. It was impossible to lose him between the naked trees that created the bones of the forest. The lake was the same distance as the cave I had made my temporary home, only in the opposite direction. As the crystal water came into view, the two residents stopped to tie up their horses.

I swooped down, landing on a tree branch above them. The demon looked up as the branch creaked.

"I don't think I've seen a crow this far away from the estate," the demon said.

The mermaid looked up at me, narrowing her eyes. "Something seems familiar about it."

"It's a crow. They all look the same."

I shifted into human form and said, "That's a little rude, isn't it?"

The mermaid yelped, clinging to her lover's arm. He tensed, going on high alert. His hand hovered over the sword strapped to his side, falling into the protector role. It had become apparent that talking to the mermaid alone was next to impossible, which meant I had to convince her and her lover to help me. The demon was one of the main guardsmen for the king. It was his responsibility to protect the estate. If he learned the real reason I had come to Ethlow, he'd never agree to help.

The demon's fingers twitched, ready to act. "Who are you?"

I kicked my feet as they dangled over the branch. "She knows."

The mermaid squinted her eyes. "You're the one who gave me the ring. The one Elcy asked us to help. Kestria, right?"

I beamed at the recognition. "I knew you'd be smart. Smarter than him." I gestured to the demon.

"Excuse me?"

"You're cute and all, but that many muscles usually means a smaller brain."

He stepped forward, his body going taut, but the mermaid placed a hand on his arm, stopping him in his tracks. He might have been loyal to the demon king, but he was whipped for the mermaid clinging to his side. If I convinced her, he'd easily follow.

"I have plenty of brains," the demon huffed.

"What's two plus two?"

The guardsman lurched forward, but the short, curvy mermaid held him back.

"Reamann," she pleaded. She stepped forward, but the demon put his hand in front of her. "Why did you follow us out here?" She was the one in charge in the relationship. There was no doubt about that.

"Elcy spoke to you. You know." She would need more from me to devote herself to my cause, but I wanted to hear her thoughts.

"You want Aukina to help you face the demon queen and put her life in danger for you?" The demon's chest heaved up and down, his eyes rife with anger.

"Yes." It was a simple answer.

"And why should she help someone she doesn't know?"

I flipped off the tree, landing in a crouch. I stood slowly, facing the demon without fear. His training was nothing compared to mine, and it wouldn't take much to end him. I wouldn't even need my weapons.

"Because she saved my life," Aukina answered before I could decide how to handle the situation. The mermaid slid between the two of us. She placed one hand on the demon's chest while facing me. "You were the one who saved my life."

I nodded once. It happened months ago. I had been surveying the estate, looking for entry points and weaknesses. Happenchance brought me to the mermaid standing up to a merchant. She had been weak with no fighting skills, but it didn't stop her from facing a dangerous male to protect something special to her friend. It was brave and stupid, and it was why I chose her.

"Why?" Aukina asked.

The real reason wouldn't give the impact I needed. "Because everyone deserves a chance to fight and live, no matter who they are." I held her gaze, breathing deeply.

"You didn't know me."

"I didn't have to." The mermaid's and demon's faces softened, and I knew my words hit their marks.

Reamann stepped to the side, facing me head on. "You would be better off asking King Zathrian for help over us. He is the one who has the power to stand against a demon queen."

I had been thinking about that problem, knowing the residents trusted the king to save them. "I could ask him for help, and I have thought about it. But if King Zathrian gets involved, it would start a war. I am bound to Queen Math'ara's service. I know how vicious she can be, which is why I know it's not fair to involve anyone else." I let my head hang, my eyes falling to the floor.

A warm hand took mine and squeezed. "We will help you."

I looked up and met soft brown eyes. I squeezed her hand back, and my chest fluttered.

"You will?" My eyes sparkled with fake hope. It was too easy to manipulate them. I let go of her hand and walked past them.

"We will," Reamann answered with a nod.

"I don't know how I'll ever thank you." I pulled my hand away from the mermaid and looked around. "So what's for lunch?" I approached the horse and rifled through the saddlebag, searching for the picnic they had packed.

"Hey, you can't look through our stuff like that." Reamann rushed towards me, but he was too late. I had already taken a container of food and walked away.

"Your girlfriend makes the best meals, and I'm not wasting an opportunity to eat her cooking."

"You like my food?" Aukina perked up. She hurried to the saddlebag and grabbed the rest of what she packed.

"It's the best in all five kingdoms. If I could eat it every day, I would be the happiest being in the world." I took a bite of a fish roll and hummed as the mix of flavors hit my tongue. Stolen food tasted better than regular food.

"That's my lunch." The demon narrowed his eyes, but he didn't sound as annoyed as I had hoped.

"I'll make you more when we get back," Aukina said. "You can have my food."

Reamann grabbed her chin, making her look up at him. "I am not taking your food. I'll starve before I let you skip a meal."

I gagged at the show of affection. It was... cute. It was also over the top. They both looked aghast at my response. "Don't worry. It was you guys. Not the food."

"When did you eat Aukina's food before, anyway?" Reamann asked, ignoring my previous comment.

I shrugged, giving myself time to chew and swallow the next bite. "When you have been on the run for as long as I have, you have to scrape by in whatever way you can. I swipe food from the kitchen here and there when possible." When the master of the house wasn't hunting me down.

"How long have you been on the run?" Aukina's brows furrowed. She was too good for the mortal realm.

I counted on my fingers. "Nine months, give or take."

"You poor thing. You've been by yourself all this time?" The creases in her forehead deepened. She took a step forward, and I carefully took a step back. I didn't want to get stuck in another hug.

"It's easier to be alone. Less pressure, you know?" I took another bite, unfazed by the mermaid's comment. The life of an assassin was a lonely one, but I had found it easier than the life of a royal. I had accompanied Myst'elle to a handful of balls and meetings, and I ended up bored out of my mind.

Both the demon and the mermaid stared at me, their eyes heavy with emotions I didn't understand. I had seen them bickering on more than one occasion. Couples constantly broke up and made the other cry. It was too difficult to deal with another's emotions.

"Good thing you don't have to be alone anymore," Reamann said. "You have two new friends."

I held back my first thought, unsure of the proper response. I wanted their help, not their friendship. "Friends?" If they thought we were friends, it'd be easier to manipulate them, but I didn't understand the tug in my chest.

"Yes, friends," Aukina agreed. "When we free you from the demon queen, you can come out of hiding and join us for lunch. I'm sure the others wouldn't mind the extra company. And then you can eat my cooking every day."

Her description was strangely appealing. Eating her food regularly sounded like the life of royalty. It was a shame it'd never come to fruition. The moment I accomplished my tasks, they would hate me, and any sense of friendship would disappear.

"That sounds nice," I said, a fake smile on my lips. There was only one friend I'd ever have. Myst'elle knew me for what I was, and she cared about me in spite of the work I did for her mother. When this was done, I would return to her, leaving a trail of broken hearts in my wake.

Chapter
10

J asper watched me from the corner of the cave, curled around
himself to maintain his heat. The clouds were dark in the sky,
blocking the sun and making it feel later than it actually was. My
wyvern huffed to get my attention, his eyes wide with worry.

"I know this is a dangerous plan, but everything I do is dangerous. I have three of them in the palm of my hands, and every second
I waste risks my secret getting out. I don't have much of a choice.
If I can't find the Aethrium Stone, then all of this would be for
nothing, and there is one being who knows where it is."

I was beginning to regret letting the pixie take the ancient artifact when I did. My calculations had been wrong. The Aethrium
Stone wasn't as easy to find as I had anticipated.

I slipped three additional rings onto my finger before tossing the
bag into the corner. Two of the rings were necessary for the plan,
and the last one hid the rest of the jewelry adorning my fingers in an
invisible force. Years ago, I discovered a magical artificer who knew
how to embed magic into items. Ever since, she had been one of my
key contacts. While my body could shift and bend into whatever
I willed it, I couldn't bend the world around me. Rings were easy

to carry, and they gave me an edge when dealing with other beings with powers.

Three additional rings were enough for my plan. I preferred having them all on me, but if everything went as expected, I'd lose anything I had on me that wasn't hidden. I tossed my tenisium daggers next, knowing those were too important to lose. Without them, taking down the demon king would have been next to impossible.

Jasper growled as I discarded my favorite gear.

I did my best to ignore his protests, but my chest ached, knowing he was upset with me. "You know what I am and what I risk every mission. I have no choice but to succeed."

Jasper turned his back to me, flapping his wings and stirring up dust in the process. I pressed my lips into a tight line. I understood he was looking out for my well being. He was the only one who'd care if I didn't come back. Myst'elle would miss me, sure, but she had plenty of other friends and responsibilities, and she was used to my absence. Without me, she'd be fine, but Jasper... He'd have nothing.

I slipped two plain daggers in place of the tenisium ones before approaching my moody wyvern. I sat next to him with my back turned and a heavy weight on my chest. "Don't worry. I'm better than some shadow demon. He may have a lifetime of skills, but he's been stuck in his ways for centuries. He's not used to a real threat, and that's what I am. A *real* threat. He will not stop me from returning to you. Nothing will."

Jasper nuzzled his nose under my hand, forcing me to pet him. I wrapped my arms around his neck and breathed deeply. I would destroy the world if it meant keeping him safe.

When I pulled back, I felt my eyes glistening. It was only temporary. I'd make sure of that. But on the microscopic chance I failed...

I took Jasper's head in my hands, feeling the dull spikes along his skull. "Listen to me. If I'm not back in a week, I want you to fly north to Mithcourt. There are dragon fae there, and they will respect you. There are even rumors that there is a dragon hiding somewhere in those mountains."

Jasper huffed, hating every word I said.

"You won't need to, but just in case..." My throat tightened. I wouldn't fail. I was too skilled for that. "Whatever you do, don't go back to Valenmae without me. Math'ara would punish you for my failure, and I refuse to let that happen."

Jasper pressed his head against my chest, knowing how vicious the demon queen was. She had punished other wyverns for failing her, making sure the other creatures saw, so they knew what fate awaited them if they failed the same way. Wyverns made for incredible mounts. They were brilliant, strong, and their wings gave an advantage over grounded creatures. I had never planned to get attached to him, knowing the risks, but Jasper had been there for me since we bonded.

"I will be back." I wasn't sure if I said that for my sake or for his. Either way, it didn't lessen the ache in my heart.

The roof was not suitable for what I had planned. It was too open and convenient. The greenhouse was too public. The stables risked animal lives. There was only one place that suited the attack I had planned, and it was insane in the best way.

I strode up to the front door, letting my hips sway with swagger. A gold ring sat in the mouth of a stone creature with a twisted face on the door. It was the final attempt to scare visitors away who weren't desperate enough to stay at the demon king's estate. The shroud of darkness was enough to drive away anyone who had another choice. Otherwise, any poor beggar would end up at the demon king's estate.

Kinzlea was littered with rumors of the demon king's vicious tales. It was a shame the kingdom didn't know that their demon king was the best of all five in the mortal realm, but the rumors were intentional, definitely started by the master of shadows. The last thing he needed was for an entire kingdom to take advantage of the kind heart of the king sitting on the throne.

I grabbed the metal ring, icy with the taste of winter, and slammed it against the wood three times. There was only ever one who answered the door of Ethlow. He was the one responsible for greeting new residents.

The door creaked open, and shadows licked the floor.

"Has anyone ever told you that your theatrics are over the top?" I grinned as the master of the house emerged from the shadows.

Viridian's muscles were carved with shock, making him unusually rigid. He said nothing as he took in my audacity. His enemy walked up to the front door and dared to smile at him. It went beyond madness. It was complete insanity.

I wiggled my fingers. "Hello? Is anyone in there? I was hoping I could take refuge in the demon king's estate. You see, I haven't had anything to eat in weeks, and I am absolutely starving. I can work for shelter. I'm particularly skilled with knives. I'd be happy to show you." I leaned in, waving my hand in front of his face, humming. "Did I break your brain?"

Shadows whipped out, snapping at my hand. Viridian bared his teeth, and the ground below my feet shook with the rage of the demon.

"You just made the biggest mistake of your life, shapeshifter."

"Or I made the best decision. The look on your face was priceless. Hordes of people would pay to see that pretty face of yours out of sorts."

Shadows snapped again, this time with more force. I barely managed to dodge, which meant it was time to run.

"Catch me if you can!" A giggle ripped from my throat as a snarl erupted from the Shadow Slinger. He was cracking at the seams, but it wasn't enough. I wanted to see the demon unleashed. My feet flew over the black stone path, aiming for the trees. The forest would provide better coverage than the front of the estate. I just had to lead the master of the house away from his precious haven.

The air shifted as the demon stepped through the shadows. I rolled onto the dead grass and was on my feet a split second later.

Shadows slashed at my body, but they failed to get through the dragon scale armor. Magic could not penetrate the ancient creature's skin. It was what led to the majestic beasts being hunted and driven to extinction—or so some rumors said. Others said there were a handful of dragons that went deep into hiding to protect what was left of their kind. Either way, it made material rare and exorbitantly expensive, but Queen Math'ara only provided the best for her pawns.

"You'll have to do better than that!"

The air pulsed with the demon's power and frustration, making my heart thrum with exhilaration. The Shadow Slinger was out of practice. He wasn't used to real challenges anymore.

I reached the gate surrounding the estate and hoisted myself over it with ease. Before my feet hit the ground, a pool of shadows covered the dirt. I shifted midair into a crow and launched forward. I couldn't make it too easy for the Shadow Slinger. When I cleared the first tree, I rolled into human form.

Viridian appeared, and it felt like slamming into a brick wall. My dagger was up before his fingers found my throat. I shifted, prepared for the next attack.

"I think you've gotten rusty with age. I have to say, I'm disappointed." I couldn't help the smirk that graced my lips. Taunting the demon was delicious.

"I am not the type to rush into a kill. I have learned patience is better than the wild antics of a young shapeshifter."

I blocked the demon's shadows with my dagger, but it wasn't as effective with my plain iron blade. "You wound me."

"I will." Viridian's sharp teeth glistened as he struck with his shadows and a dagger at the same time.

I blocked his weapon and twisted my body unnaturally, avoiding both attacks. I quickly countered with an attack of my own. My weapon was aimed at his side, and as he blocked it, my foot flung around, making contact with his face.

Before I could delight in the pain of his failure, he disappeared into the shadows. Arms wrapped around me from behind, one around my waist and one around my neck. I kicked my feet up, and when they landed on the ground, I used my thigh muscles to flip the demon over my back. He held onto me, bringing me flying with him. His back hit the ground with a thump, but he kept me caged in his arms.

"The games are over, shapeshifter," he growled in my ear. He was so close to shattering, but he wasn't there yet.

Viridian tightened his grip on my neck, closing my windpipe and making it impossible to breathe. I struggled against him, but his grip was ironclad. I had thirty seconds before I lost too much strength to break free. A needle pricked my neck, and a heaviness ran through my veins, sinking into my bones. I thrashed, knowing if I didn't break free soon, it'd be too late. I tried to shift into another form after thirty-one seconds.

"I don't think so." Shadows slammed against my face, and everything went dark as I lost consciousness.

Chapter

II

The dampness of the floor pressed into my skin. The air was sticky and tasted old. I didn't move for several minutes, waiting for my head to stop pounding. A steady drip mixed with rushing water in the distance—sounds I was unfamiliar with. Wherever the Shadow Slinger had taken me wasn't part of the main estate. There were no signs of life, which meant I was alone. For now.

I pushed myself up, my body stiff from the cold. My fur lined dragon armor was gone, replaced by itchy cotton that did nothing to shape the curves of my body or warm my skin. My weapons were missing. So were my boots with the steel blade hidden in the sole. I breathed slowly, forcing the air into my nose. I didn't want the rancid air to coat my tongue.

I tested each limb for signs of injuries. Bruises riddled my legs, and my ribs ached where the demon had had his arm wrapped around my waist. There was a similar bruise on my neck. The injuries told me I had been out for less than twelve hours. In another twelve, the bruises would be gone, erasing the evidence of the fight with the Shadow Slinger.

The pounding in my head refused to subside. I pushed through the aches in my body, grateful I was alive. It had been a gamble. The Shadow Slinger could have killed me, ending everything, but I had seen the look in his eyes from our fight a few days ago. As furious as he was, he was also impressed. I had banked on that meaning he wouldn't outright kill me. The challenge was as delicious to him as it was to me—or he planned on torturing me for information. Either way, I had been 99.5 percent certain the fight wouldn't have ended in my death.

The gamble paid off, but the problem was I didn't know where I was. Metal bars surrounded me in a cube barely big enough for me to lie stretched out. Several identical chambers sat next to mine, but they were all empty. Stones lined the walls and floors, and a small stream of water weaved its way over a worn out tunnel outside my prison cell. The water fed the glowing blue and green moss that covered the walls and ceiling in patches.

The moss was the only form of light in the dark tunnels. I tried to shift my eyes into that of an owl to get a clearer image of my surroundings, but the throbbing in my head increased. I glanced at the crook of my elbow. A pin prick had been left behind, matching the one on my neck. Two injections had been given to me. The first to subdue me and the second to stop my transformations.

I grinned, pleased by the Shadow Slinger's foresight. I grabbed the bars, testing them next. They were made of solid iron, which might have done something to contain a regular magic user, but iron did nothing to my powers. A shapeshifter's magic was different from the magic most beings used. Iron could subdue fae, elves, and witches—although the extent varied based on thickness and quality of the iron and the strength of a magic user. These bars would limit the powers of some of the strongest beings.

I reached through the bars. Electricity jolted my fingers, forcing my body to lurch back. The master of the house thought of everything. Even if the drugs in my system wore off, there was an extra shield around the cell, preventing me from shifting into a creature small enough to slip free.

I laughed at the situation. It was more decadent than I had anticipated. It would make my escape that much sweeter.

It was impossible to tell how much time had passed in the dark prison cell. There were no windows to indicate the time of day. There was nothing to entertain myself with, especially without being able to shift forms. The only thing that distinguished time was the growl in my stomach, but even that subsided to a dull ache after a while.

When shadows shifted, I jumped to my feet and grabbed the metal containing me, careful to not touch the magical field. The throb in my head had dulled, the drugs making their way through my body. It'd be another hour before it cleared my system, maybe less if I was lucky.

I hoped the shadow demon miscalculated how much of the poison to inject me with. Shapeshifters were rare, and we made a point to keep facts about us a secret—at least I did, even to my queen. I had never met another shapeshifter, which only added to my theory. It meant that it wasn't common knowledge that shapeshifters' bodies burned through drugs, poisons, and other forms of impairment at unusual speeds. It made it impossible to indulge in the effects alcohol provided, not that I had an interest in that. I liked keeping my mind sharp. In my line of work, there was no telling who was ready to stab me in the back when I let my defenses down.

Shadows formed a body, and Viridian's usual composure was intact. It was only temporary. I gave him a false win to let his guard down.

"It's about time you visited," I said. "It's rude to leave your guests without entertainment for hours on end."

"It's been three hours." His voice was flat, the previous irritation gone.

"Three hours? I would have guessed three days." I leaned forward, pressing my chest against the bars as I arched my back. I wasn't gifted with anything significant in the breast department. They were smaller than average, which I hated for a long time. Part of me still hated it, but it made many jobs easier, so I had learned to accept it. Mostly.

The demon's brow quirked. "Has anyone ever taught you to be patient?"

I was plenty patient when it mattered—like when I had to spend a good portion of the year at Ethlow, stalking my enemies to learn their weaknesses. "Has anyone ever taught you manners?" I quipped back. It was better that the shadow demon never learned

the extent my patience went. "And where's dinner? I'm starving."
My mouth salivated as I thought about Aukina's cooking.

"You don't seem to comprehend that you're my prisoner. You
don't get the luxury of food and entertainment." The Shadow
Slinger was enjoying this. Good. I'd let him have his fun for now.

"I'm telling you now that I am absolutely useless without a good
meal in my stomach. You can torture me all you want, but I won't
tell you anything until my stomach is full of the best food in the
estate." My eyes twinkled as ire flashed in the demon's eyes. It was
a bluff I hoped he'd take. I wouldn't tell him anything, even with
a full stomach.

"You are infuriating." His tone was flat, but the twitch in his eye
gave away the irritation slowly building.

"You like being in control, and you hate that you can't control
me. Nothing you could do to me would ever subdue me." I looked
him up and down, taking in the width of his shoulders and the
cake that was nicely shaped behind him. "Well, there might be one
thing you could do to subdue me. That's assuming you know your
way around a female body, which is doubtful."

Viridian stepped forward, clasping his hands behind his back.
His horns fluttered as he leaned in, leaving the magical barrier and
bars between us. "You couldn't handle the things I'd do to you."

Warmth bloomed in my chest. I hadn't expected him to flirt
back. His perfect facade was cracking, and it wouldn't be long
before I saw what it was like for him to let loose.

"It's you who can't handle me. You had to lock me up and drug me to make sure I didn't slip through your fingers. Admit it. I am the most challenging opponent you have ever faced."

The Shadow Slinger stepped back, shadows crawling over his skin. He was about to disappear, the opposite of what I wanted.

My grip on the metal tightened. "Where are you going?"

"To get you food, so you can do something else with your mouth other than talk."

"There are other things I can put in my mouth to stop me from talking." I winked, and the demon disappeared without a response.

Viridian wasn't gone long, but when he returned, I had settled on the floor with my back against the wall. The smell of garlic hit my nose, and my body perked up. The demon held a plate in one hand like a skilled butler.

The promise of food had me on my feet and drooling. "That looks incredible? Did the mermaid make it? I love her food."

"Miss Aukina is not the only one who can cook." There was a hint of pride in his voice, easily missed by someone without training.

"You made that?" I eyed the plate. It was some sort of chicken dish with tomato sauce and vegetables, and the scent alone was almost enough to make me pant.

"I did, and if you want any, you'll have to answer my questions."

Oh, he was good. Using the direct line to my heart to get me to talk. If he wanted answers, I'd give them to him. "Game on, pretty boy."

"This isn't a game." The light in his eyes contradicted his words.

"Everything is a game. Tell me the rules, and I'll play." I leaned against the wall and crossed my arms, acting nonchalant. The more he knew I wanted the food, the more power it gave him over me.

"Answer my question, and you'll get a bite of food."

"There's a shield separating us."

Viridian waved his hand, and the invisible shield fell. If I had the ability to transform, it would've been the perfect opportunity to escape—not that I was ready to do that.

"If I answer one of your questions, I get a bite of food, and you have to answer a question of mine."

"This is not a negotiation."

"If you are going to try to get to know me, then I want to learn more about you. Food is not enough of a motivator." I inspected my nails, knowing he couldn't sense the lie on my tongue. Lying had become second nature to me. The role of assassin forced me to take on personas that did not belong to me. There were times when it was difficult to know what was mine and what was borrowed.

I anticipated the demon's rejection, but instead, he said, "Fine, but I won't answer questions that cross lines."

"Same."

He took a slow breath to steady himself. His sense of control was failing, making his irritation return in full force. "Why are you here?"

"If I recall correctly, a certain demon choked me out, drugged me, and then threw me into a magically warded prison." I smirked, knowing the effect my answer had on him.

"That's not what I meant."

"I answered your question honestly. It's not my fault you didn't choose your words wisely. I'm a bit disappointed. I expected better from someone so old." I crossed the room and grabbed the bars, stretching my fingers to test if the shield was properly removed. "Now, where's my bite of food? Unless you're the type to go back on your word."

Viridian didn't deign a response. He cut a piece of chicken with a fork and held it out to me. I took the food before carefully licking my lips clean. I let out a long moan as the flavors hit my tongue. The demon's cooking was much better than the mermaid's—something I didn't think possible.

"Where did you learn to cook?"

"I taught myself to cook. I must be the best at everything I put my mind to."

"Everything?" I lifted my brows, my mind going to dangerous places.

He ignored my follow up question. "Why did Queen Math'ara send you to Ethlow?"

"She wants the power your king recently obtained, the power he's planning on keeping to himself. Kinzlea is not the only kingdom suffering."

There was no shock on his face, like I had hoped. "If Queen Math'ara wanted the Aethrium Stone, she should have sent someone to retrieve it."

She did, but I didn't tell him that. "The Aethrium Stone?" I let the words roll over my tongue. "So that's what she wanted."

"Don't act like you didn't know that."

"Believe it or not, I'm not always told the specific details of my missions. The demon queen likes to keep her plans private, which means giving her soldiers as little information as possible." It wasn't a total lie. There were many times I was sent in blind to a situation, expected to figure it out on my own. Luckily, I had my ways of finding out information before the queen even assigned me a task.

"I don't believe it."

I shrugged. "That's your prerogative. Now where's my bite?"

He hesitated, debating about denying me. Then he lifted another bite to my lips. I let out another moan. After a day of not eating, the food tasted better than ever.

"Where is your king keeping the Aethrium Stone?" I asked with a mouth full of food.

The shadow demon's eyes flickered. "What makes you think I would answer you?"

I knew he wouldn't answer my question. "Because you think I'm endearing. That's your question, so I get another."

"That's not how this works." He cut a piece of chicken and held it out of my reach. "I'm not surprised Queen Math'ara knows about the Aethrium Stone, but why did she send the Infernal Dagger, the best assassin in the mortal realms, to retrieve it? She could have sent a thief."

I pressed my hand against my chest and fluttered my eyes. "You think I'm the best assassin? I appreciate you for seeing true talent."

"Answer me, Kestria."

There it was again. My name on his tongue. I tilted my head slowly, taking in the demon. It was rare to hear my name on another's lips, but there was something special about the way he spoke it. "I am an assassin. I am a thief. I am a spy. I am whatever my queen demands of me. I am a shapeshifter in more ways than my physical body."

Viridian held out the fork. I wrapped my lips around the metal, refusing to break eye contact with my enemy. The demon needed to be in control. He might have been bound to the demon king, but he was the one that ran Ethlow. He kept the estate safe, pulling strings behind the scene. "You have the Aethrium Stone." It made perfect sense. The master of the house wouldn't trust the king to protect a precious artifact.

"What else are you planning?" The demon ignored my statement, only confirming my suspicions.

"I am planning on leaving this estate as soon as possible. You see, I have hordes of friends waiting for my return. They miss me dearly. As you probably know, I am the life of a party. Life must be rather dull in the Valenmae royal courts without me. I also plan on stealing at least one more meal from the kitchen. You found talent in that mermaid. I hope you appreciate her. I also plan—"

"I'm not interested in your antics," he growled.

"I was only answering your question."

"Are you here to hurt King Zathrian?"

"You already asked me a question. It's my turn, and where's my food?" I waited for my bite before diving into my next inquiry. "How many beings have you slept with?"

"I'm not answering that."

"That many, or that few?" I challenged. I wasn't sure which answer I wanted to hear more. There were appeals to both.

"Why do you care?"

"Answer my question, and I'll answer yours."

Viridian cut another chunk of chicken and practically shoved it into my mouth. "You are infuriating."

"And you are an absolute peach," I said with a full mouth.

"Why can't you take anything seriously?" The fractures in his facade were shining. It was time to try to push him over the edge.

I reached through the gate, grabbing the hem of his pants. I pulled the demon closer to the metal bars, and he let me. "Because when you work for the demon queen, living life on a line between death and danger, you learn to have fun where you can. You should learn a thing or two from me."

I slipped my hand into his pants and felt for the part I hadn't been able to stop thinking about. He hardened beneath my touch, and a low growl escaped as I wrapped my fingers around his cock.

Chapter
12

"What the fuck do you think you're doing?" His breathy voice stroked a nerve I didn't think I had.

He didn't stop me, so I tightened my grip. "Teaching you to have fun." I moved my hand up and down, testing to see how far he'd let me go. My heart thundered in my chest as the Shadow Slinger gripped the bars and leaned closer to the cage.

"If you're going to do it, do it right." His teal eyes darkened as he looked down at me.

I grinned, ignoring the wobble in my legs. "As you wish." I yanked him closer and unbuttoned his pants, pulling his cock free. My hand moved up and down, feeling his shaft thicken as he hardened further. His eyes fluttered shut, his breath growing shallow. "Someone has a lot of pent up frustration," I teased.

His eyes snapped open. "You said there was another way to preoccupy that mouth of yours. Show me."

I could've argued with him, pushed him to the limit, but my knees sank to the ground, maintaining eye contact with the demon the entire time. If he wanted me to show him what I was capable of, I'd do just that.

I gripped his cock and licked the tip. He wasn't like the other mortals I had been with. The ridges along the shaft were the kind that only belonged to demons. As I swirled my tongue along his length, he hissed, making my blood pulse. I loved the way he reacted to my tongue, and I wanted to watch him come undone beneath my touch. I licked down and then up, pausing at the tip. Irritation flashed in his eyes. I was taking too long. I moved deliberately slow, and he bucked his hips. His desperation dripped from his body, and I wanted to take advantage of it.

"It's been a while since someone has been on their knees for you, hasn't it, Shadow Slinger?" Before he could respond, I wrapped my lips over the tip of his cock and took as much of him into my mouth as I could.

Instead of a snarky comment, he groaned, his head falling back at the sensation of my mouth wrapped around him. I moved up and down his shaft, sucking him in to add pressure. His knuckles turned white as he gripped the bars, the metal threatening to buckle under his grasp. He bit his lower lip to stop himself from emitting unwanted noises, but when I added my hand with my mouth, he couldn't stop the groans that rumbled from deep within his chest. If I kept my pace, I would break his beast free from the cage he kept it in, and I needed that more than air.

If that was the way to get the demon to let his defenses fall, then I would do whatever it took. It had nothing to do with the steady pulse between my legs. I needed to see him come undone and use the moment of weakness to get what I wanted.

I pulled back to take a breath, but Viridian's hands threaded through my hair, refusing to let me move. He thrusted into my mouth, and any sense of control I had disappeared. The ache between my legs grew as the master of the house used me to get himself off. He was close. I could tell by the way his breathing bounced off the brick walls. Another thirty seconds, and he'd fall over an edge neither of us could come back from.

Each thrust grew needier and more desperate, and after twenty-five seconds, I grabbed his wrist, twisting his hand free from my head. I was on my feet a second later, putting distance between us. Viridian straightened his neck, and when our eyes met, my throat went dry. The darkness in his eyes went beyond the irritation I had become skilled at weaving. It was need and frustration on the deepest level. The look alone was almost enough to put me back on my knees.

I wiped my mouth and held his eyes. "Too bad I'm locked in here and can't finish you off. I'm sure you need a good lay to loosen those shoulders."

Viridian disappeared in the shadows, and his hand clasped around my neck a second later. He slammed me against the wall, his shadows pinning my wrists above my head. "I'm not done with you yet."

His mouth slammed against mine in a fervor. He nipped my lip, drawing blood. The pain was beyond delicious, and I couldn't hold back my moan. The demon's tongue swiped over my mouth, and I opened for him. I was putty in his shadows, unable to think long enough to pull myself together.

Viridian let go of my neck and grabbed my breast, kneading it roughly. His lips grazed over my throat before his teeth pierced my skin. If I didn't know better, I would have thought he was claiming me, but the demon had no reason for that. We were enemies, and I'd never be his. It didn't stop my hips from bucking forward, needing more than I had imagined.

His tongue ran over the blood that dripped down my neck. I writhed beneath him, my senses gone. It had been too long since another touched me, and it had never felt like that. It was confusing. This wasn't supposed to be about my pleasure.

"I like seeing you squirm." His voice caressed my ear, melting my bones. If I could shift, I would have become a puddle on the floor.

Viridian ran a claw over my torso, starting from my clavicle and moving down to my navel, splitting the threads of my shirt. The cool air hit my chest, but the demon's lips found my nipple, taking it into his mouth without hesitation. I arched into the feeling, the ache between my legs unbearable.

Either the Shadow Slinger sensed my need, or his own became too much for him. With a couple of carefully placed swipes, my pants fell free, leaving scratches behind from his claws. I was exposed to him, vulnerable to his every desire while he was fully clothed. It didn't matter that I was the one who started this. He was in charge, and we both knew it.

His shadows yanked on my wrists, pulling me higher until my feet dangled in the air. Viridian hooked his shoulders under my legs and dove into my center. As the warmth of his mouth found the apex of my thighs, my vision went black. He sucked on my clit, finding it immediately. His fingers pushed into my entrance, hitting the most sensitive spot. The pressure in my core built quickly, and there was no doubt his previous statement was true. The demon knew *exactly* how to pleasure a woman, and it felt fucking amazing.

I rolled my hips, adding to the friction and trying to take back a semblance of control. I was close. My body stood on the edge of a precipice, and only a few more flicks of a tongue would push me into pure bliss.

Viridian pulled back, cool air replacing his warmth as his shadows held me in place. The desire in my core turned to pain without the release of pleasure that had been teased.

"It's unfortunate I don't have the time to finish you off, shapeshifter." His lips tugged into a smirk, something I hadn't realized was possible for the stone-faced demon.

My chest heaved, and I saw red. I was his prisoner, but he wasn't going to defeat me like that. I swung my hips forward, wrapping my legs around his waist and yanking him towards me. He disappeared along with his shadows. I landed on the floor in a crouch. The hair on the back of my neck stood on end. The demon hadn't gone far, lingering in hidden shadows.

"Are you going to leave like a coward? Unable to finish the job. I thought you'd be a completionist." It was stupid to taunt the demon. I was trapped in a cell with no way out.

"Is that your question?" His voice floated in the air, but he didn't materialize.

"Is that yours?"

"You don't know when to stop talking, shapeshifter. You are at my mercy, and I could kill you in seconds, yet you keep running that beautiful mouth of yours."

"This isn't my first time in a cage. What can I say? I get restless. I'd rather have company like you than be left alone." I tracked the shadows flickering in the corners of my eyes, buying time.

"Who managed to lock *you* in a cage?"

My heart moved at a steady pace, but there was a pit at the base of my stomach. "If I answer, do I get my treat?"

"I'll consider it."

There were two paths I could take. The truth or an utter lie. There was only one that would matter to the Shadow Slinger. "Queen Math'ara did, right before she gave me this mark." I turned, revealing the tattoo of the spike vine with a bleeding rose.

Viridian's fingers trace my bare back, following the curves of the vines. "You chose to work for the demon queen."

"I chose to live. With Queen Math'ara, you either agree to her terms, or she locks you away in a cage and lets you die a slow, painful death." I turned, not afraid to look the demon in the eyes. Sympathy was the last thing Viridian would give, especially knowing my soul was tied to the enemy of his king. "Where's my treat?"

Viridian grabbed the back of my head and pulled me into a hungry kiss. Our tongues tangled, his sweetness erasing memories. He grabbed the back of my hair and pulled my head back to expose my neck. He nipped at the skin, leaving little marks along the sensitive areas.

He grabbed my hips and hoisted me up. My back hit the wall a second later. With the help of his shadows, he adjusted himself at my entrance before pulling me down onto him in a swift motion. I cried out as he filled me completely. His movements were unrelenting. There was nothing gentle about his touch, and it made me want more.

The demon's hips were powerful, but it was more than that. His shadows stroked my body, overwhelming my senses. After nearly bringing me to the edge, my nerves were on fire. The pressure exploded like a wildfire, crawling over my skin in rapid waves. He chased his own pleasure, stilling only after spilling into me.

I clung to his neck as our chests heaved in an attempt to catch our breaths.

"I'll give you credit, pretty boy. You have more skills than I thought." I brushed my thumb over the ring on my middle finger, feeling for the nearly invisible button.

"You have also impressed me, shapeshifter."

"It's almost a shame we work for enemies. We could have made a great team." I pressed the button, and the ring molded into the shape of a miniature dagger. Without giving the demon a chance to respond, I jammed the weapon between his ribs, twisting it to ensure the poison went straight for his heart.

Viridian's entire body tensed. "What did you do?"

I untangled myself from him, letting my feet land on the ground silently. The demon tried to grab me, but I stepped away from him with ease. His muscles wound tighter and tighter until they were too rigid to move. "Don't worry. It won't kill you. You will be paralyzed for at least a day, giving me plenty of time to search your precious estate without trouble."

Viridian's eyes burned with hatred and betrayal, and I couldn't help the laugh that filled the air. "When I asked for a treat, I wanted more chicken, but thanks for the orgasm. Oh, I guess I need clothes too."

I took his shirt but left his pants behind—despite my temptation to see him naked. It wasn't fun when the other person couldn't move. "I suppose this will do. Tata, Shadow Slinger. Have fun sleeping in a dungeon tonight." I wiggled my fingers goodbye.

I reached for my powers and felt a flicker, enough to shift into a small creature for a few seconds. As a rat, I slipped through the bars before returning to human form and pulling on the stolen shirt. A roar followed as I dashed through the catacombs, making my skin burn with satisfaction. This time, I won.

Chapter 13

The catacombs twisted and turned beneath the castle as I left the master of the house in the prison cell. I didn't dare to look back, not wanting to deal with unwanted feelings. In all the different scenarios I crafted prior to executing my plan, that hadn't been in a single one of them. It was impossible to deny the attractiveness of the Shadow Slinger. I loved a male who took pride in his appearance. Viridian was dressed to perfection, but sleeping with the enemy was a dangerous line to walk. I knew that, yet seeing his composure break, even for a brief moment, left something stirring deep within me.

I ignored that feeling, focusing on navigating the dark hallways. The Aethrium Stone was waiting for me to find it before the poison wore off and the Shadow Slinger came after me with a vengeance. After what I had done, I had no doubt the demon would attempt to kill me. Every other attempt had been a dangerous dance to learn more about one another and nothing more, but the game had changed.

The stream of water wearing down the stone path led the way out of the maze, twisting and turning through complex hallways until it led to a rusted metal ladder with the rungs embedded into the stone walls. It was slick with water, and my body groaned from the exertion it took to climb to freedom. Between the poison lingering in my system, sleeping on the hard floor, and whatever happened between the Shadow Slinger and me, I was running on fumes.

A latched grate at the top of the ladder opened to the horses' troughs. The pipe meant to refill the animals' drinking water was leaking, which explained the stream that made its way through the catacomb.

The sun slipped behind the mountains, giving minutes to get inside before creatures of the underworld emerged and threatened my life. I wasn't in a condition to fight any beasts. I didn't have the reserves to transform again, which meant I was entering the estate in human form. It was riskier that way, but with the master of the house otherwise preoccupied, I wasn't concerned.

I slipped through the halls, relying on every piece of training I had to avoid unwanted attention. The hallways were mostly empty, except for a few residents meandering to their private quarters. The door with moths and other bugs carved directly into the wood was unlocked, making it easy to slip inside.

The healer wasn't in the infirmary, leaving me alone with the pinned bugs covering the wall. It was the only type of decoration the vampire had. I went to the cabinet filled with potions and salves and rifled through it, looking for two different concoctions. The glass bottles lacked labels, which made it more difficult to find what I wanted. I had to pull out the cork stoppers and unscrew lids and take a whiff of each one to distinguish what was inside.

As a child, I had been trained in toxicology. Queen Math'ara even went as far as to microdose me with poisons over the years to improve my tolerance for anything someone might try on me. It countered the effectiveness of the Shadow Slinger's drugs, making him underestimate my abilities. Between that and tending to my wounds over the years, I had become a pro with potions, tonics, and poisons.

A bottle fell, spilling the contents onto the shelf. I tensed, my hands shaking more than I was used to. It was rare for someone to weaken me like the Shadow Slinger did, but I refused to let him frazzle me. I had a job to do, and the clock was ticking.

"Satella, what are you—" The voice stopped me in my tracks.

There was no use running, since I was caught red-handed. I turned slowly, unable to hide tonics in my lack of clothing.

The door swung shut as a wide-eyed human stared at me. Her long brown hair was pulled back into a ponytail, and she wore simple clothes to cover her plush body. Her dark blue eyes held a mix of fear and shock. She was cute, but she was also the worst person to walk in on me. If she called for her demon lover, it'd be over.

I should've heard her, but I had been too wrapped up with searching for a healing potion to notice. It was the mistake of an amateur. The encounter with the shadow demon threw me off more than I had realized.

"Nyri, right?" I met her eyes and smiled to disarm her.

"Do I know you?" She pressed her lips together as she searched through her memories. As the demon king's lover, she took pride in learning the names of the other residents.

"We've met before, but I looked a little different."

The human looked me up and down, taking in my disheveled appearance. My body was covered in scrapes, bruises, and dirt, and I likely looked worse than I had been imagining.

"You're hurt." She swallowed hard, concern filling her doe eyes.

"Hence coming to the infirmary." My voice was dry with sarcasm, which wasn't my usual tone. I wasn't feeling like myself for several reasons. "Satella isn't here, so I thought I'd help myself."

She nodded, seeming to accept the answer. "Who are you?"

"I'm Kestria."

Recognition flashed on her face. "The one Elcy told us about."

I nodded once. There was a 75 percent chance she had already told the demon king about me, despite Elcy asking her to keep quiet. Each day that passed only increased those odds.

The human crossed the room and gently took my hand. "Come with me." She pulled me along behind her with more confidence than I expected from a human.

"Where?" I prepared to pull away from her and run.

"You're injured and missing clothes. I'm going to help you."

I followed behind her silently, surprised she was willing to help a stranger. I didn't let my guard down. I could kill her without weapons or the ability to shapeshift if she tried anything. Despite her saying she was going to help, there was a 50 percent chance she was lying and bringing me directly to the demon king.

She led me up the black stairs with the gold railing, and I prepared to flee. I didn't risk everything to lock up the shadow demon, only to be brought to the demon king. The king was easier to manipulate, but it wasn't worth it. As we neared two large, black doors with gold swirls on it, I dug my heels into the marble floors, refusing to move another inch.

The human looked back at me. "Zath isn't in the room right now, and he said he won't be back for the rest of the night. He won't walk in on us and discover you. I promise." There were none of the typical signs of lies written on her body, but it didn't help my hesitation. As if sensing that, she continued, "You can go, if you want. I won't force you to do anything you don't want to. I may not understand why you don't want Zath's help, but I respect it."

"You haven't told him about me?" I needed to hear her say it out loud—not that it'd make me trust her more.

Her breath was ragged. "No."

"Why?"

"I'll explain inside while I clean you up. That way, no one accidentally runs into us."

There was a part of me that wanted to run away. I didn't need the human to take care of me or dress my wounds. I didn't need anyone to help me. Only I did. I needed her to get on board with my plan, and soon. This was the perfect opportunity, even if there was a 50 percent chance this was a trap.

I let her lead me into the demon king's bedroom. The doors shut behind us, and she released my hand, rushing to a conjoining room. The bed was enormous, but the room was large enough to accommodate the size. Flowers carved into the wood decorated the frame and poles that towered towards the ceiling. I ran my fingers over the dips and curves of the carvings, enjoying the smoothness brushing against the pad of my finger.

"Beautiful, isn't it?" The human emerged from the other room with a tray filled with towels, bowls of liquid, bandages, and a few other things.

"It's not the kind of thing I'd expect a demon king to have." I had been in the demon king's room several times, but I hadn't had time to take in the decorations.

"I think it's fate." A soft smile graced the human's lips. "Those are bleeding heart lilies carved on his bedposts, and that flower brought the two of us together."

Bleeding heart lilies were rare in the mortal realms. They originated from a small island in the Hallow Seas, but an ice storm wiped out most of them a decade back. Despite that, the greenhouse flourished with the magical flower. If Queen Math'ara learned the king of Kinzlea had something of that rarity, she would demand it for herself.

"I don't believe in fate. The future is crafted by each choice we make. Flowers didn't bring the two of you together. You did by choosing him."

I waited for her smile to fade, but it held steady. "That's a romantic way of thinking about it."

It wasn't what I had intended, but telling her that wouldn't pop the bubble of love she was floating in. "If you love the demon king that much, why haven't you told him about me?"

She took a slow breath, her internal struggle reflecting on her features. "Sit." She motioned to the bed. She dipped the washcloth into a bowl of warm water before slowly wiping blood and dirt off me. It was strange to have someone else take care of me. I didn't know what to make of it. "I love Zathrian more than I thought I would love anyone, but he keeps his secrets. He's afraid to worry me, or he's afraid that if I know how much danger Ethlow truly is in, it will put me in more danger. Sometimes I wish he'd be more forthcoming. I'm not as fragile as he thinks."

She pressed her lips together, taking a moment to focus on cleaning me up. She placed salves and bandages on my cuts, but her thoughts were written on her face.

"Trouble in paradise?" I prompted. If there were issues between the human and the demon king, it'd make my job easier.

She set the tray down and let out a long sigh. "Not trouble, exactly. I love him."

"But?"

She tapped her fingers, as if debating about divulging her inner secrets to a stranger. It was something I would have never done, but the human struggled to keep her mouth shut. "But he's constantly away, and he's always keeping secrets. When he is here, he is attentive and loving, but it's lonelier being with a demon king than I expected. It often feels like I'm his dirty little secret." Her eyes glistened as the words tumbled out. She hadn't told anyone this information before, but she chose to tell a spymaster, assassin, and thief.

"Have you told him you felt that way?" Relationships were too complicated—not that I had ever been in a proper one. As a child, Queen Math'ara made it clear that any relationship I devoted myself to would have ended in disaster. Relationships were distractions and weaknesses for an assassin.

The human wiped her eyes. "No. I can't add to his problems. The kingdom is in danger, and he has enough to worry about, which is why your secret is safe with me. If you need my help, you have it, and I swear I won't tell Zath about you as long as you promise it won't cause any harm to the residents at Ethlow."

Convincing the demon king's lover was easier than I had expected. I didn't have to do anything, since she managed to convince herself. All I had to do was make a hollow promise. I hesitated. Nyri helped me when she had no reason to, and she promised to keep my secret. "I promise," I said. I had to do whatever it took to complete the task set forth for me. I had those I needed to protect, and sympathy had no place in my heart.

Nyri smiled. "Good. Now, let me get you new clothes. I don't have anything your size, but it'll be better than nothing."

She pulled out a simple shirt and a pair of pants. The shirt hung loosely around me, but it was soft. The pants were too big for my hips, but with a rope, we were able to make it work. I glanced in the mirror, not recognizing myself. The cuts and bruises were part of the job, but the simple clothes made me look like a simple human—nothing like a shapeshifting assassin.

"Sorry. I don't have anything smaller," Nyri said. She licked her lips, avoiding my eyes. She was embarrassed by the size of her clothes, but she had no reason to be. She was beautiful. Her curves only added to that beauty.

"I appreciate your help. I need to go, but I'll see you soon." I opened the door, but paused, looking back at the human. "Things might be difficult with the demon you love, but treasure every second you have with him. You never know when time will run out for the two of you."

I slipped out the door, an unfamiliar weight pressing against my chest. It had been a strange night. That was all.

Chapter 14

I walked through the halls of Ethlow like I belonged. Knowing the master of the house and the demon king were otherwise preoccupied, a false sense of safety washed over me. Even if I passed by a resident, they would think nothing of my presence if I moved with confidence.

There was an area of the estate that I hadn't dared to search in the months I scouted the place: the Shadow Slinger's quarters. The one time I had approached it, wards burned the air in warning. Entering would have resulted in the magic alerting the shadow demon. It would have made any attempt to search his room futile.

Knowing he was stuck in his own prison cell as the paralytic worked through his system gave me time for a proper search. The door to Viridian's room was plain black. It was the only undecorated door in the entire estate, but it was fitting for the demon. The lock was easy to pick with the ring with hidden needles.

The door swung open, and I hesitated, waiting for spikes to shoot from the ceiling or some other deadly trap to go off. Magic crawled over the room from floors to ceiling, but it was the remnants of shadows, ready to report any ongoings that occurred while Viridian was away. The room was void of traps, likely because of the residents in the estate. If an unsuspecting resident got hurt because they crossed a boundary, it'd cause more issues than it was worth for the master of the house.

I slipped inside, and the hair on the back of my head raised. The room smelled of leather and antiseptic, immediately bringing up memories of only a few hours prior when the shadow demon had been plunged deep inside of me. I pushed those memories away, focusing on the task. I couldn't afford any other distractions. If the paralytic wore off early, I wasn't in the condition to face the Shadow Slinger.

The room was immaculate. There wasn't a speck of dust in sight, and the walls were void of decorations. He wasn't the type to put meaning into disposable objects. Only the bare minimum was required. It was cold, like the shadow demon appeared to be, but I knew the truth. He wore a mask like me. When working for one of the demon rulers, the only option was perfection.

I searched the drawers, intentionally messing up the perfectly folded clothes. The wardrobe held nothing of significance. The connected washroom lacked ancient artifacts that could save kingdoms. Unsure of where else to look, I plopped on the bed, ruffling the blanket and sheets. The bed was surprisingly comfortable, despite it looking like a bed of bricks.

Viridian wasn't a demon that slept much, if at all. The more powerful demons didn't need sleep like other mortals. They could function on only an hour or two of sleep, thriving on the life force of those they made bargains with. Some claimed they never slept at all, but those were usually the demons that needed several hours to function. They liked to lie to make themselves seem above others, but an assassin always learned the truth. The Shadow Slinger wasn't the type to lie about that. He didn't need to.

If he said he needed thirty seconds of sleep, I'd believe him. Unlike me, he had no reason to spill lies. If there was something he didn't want to talk about, he ignored the topic. He didn't use manipulation to accomplish his goals. I admired him for that. He likely hated me for my deception. If he didn't, he would before I left Ethlow with him as my prisoner.

I closed my eyes, giving into my exhaustion for a moment. Time was waning, and the pressure of success only increased with each minute that passed. With a deep breath, I focused on senses other than sight. A dull thrum pulsed beneath me. It was hardly there. Someone who wasn't attuned to magic wouldn't have noticed it, but it moved like waves, rising slowly until it crashed.

I flipped to my feet before lowering onto my stomach. My fingers brushed over the ridged wood flooring beneath the bed until I found a small divot. A piece of wood lifted, and inside there was a stone box. It took strength I barely had to lift the container. The lid scraped against the stone until it revealed the opal stone attached to a gold necklace. The ancient powers made my blood thrum, begging my fingers to wrap around it.

I snatched it from the black velvet coating the inside of the box before slipping the stone container back to its original location. The amulet called out to me, asking me to put it on. The power of the ancient artifact was undeniable, and it was tempting to slide it around my neck and taste the power, but there was one thing that held me back. No one touched what belonged to Queen Math'ara.

Clouds blocked the rising sun, darker than they had been for the past few days. I flew over the forest, eager to return to Jasper, so he knew I was okay. I was exhausted, but that was normal for me. The role of assassin required many long nights, and there wasn't always time to sleep. I could spare a few hours before returning to the estate, but I needed to speak to the librarian to ensure she was willing to help me. Then I'd be able to put the final touches on the plan and be rid of the demon king's estate and everyone in it.

As I reached the opening of the cave, I shifted into human form, missing the clothes Nyri had given to me. Without my dragon scale armor, my clothes didn't shift with me, but I had a spare outfit stored in the cave. It wasn't as high quality as the one the Shadow Slinger stole from me, but it would prevent me from ending up naked after transforming.

When my feet hit the ground, I froze, staring at the group of dragonflies hovering at the entrance of the cave. I forced my heart to slow with an invisible breath. I approached the dragonflies with a face made of stone. I bowed my head, waiting.

"I expect better from you." The dragonflies spoke, mimicking the voice of the queen, but it was distorted by the tiny voices speaking as one. Few could understand dragonflies like me. After spending enough time in a specific animal form, I picked up their language. Queen Math'ara could control the bugs, speaking through them like little puppets, and I was the only one who would understand. It was the perfect way to pass encoded messages.

"Everything is nearly set up for my plan." Excuses for why I had taken the better part of a year to defeat Queen Math'ara's enemy wouldn't matter. The queen knew the difficulty of the task. There was a reason she spent twenty-five years shaping me into a weapon. If killing a demon king was easy, she would have done it centuries ago.

"I expected you back by now. I didn't spend infinite resources on you for you to waste my time. Do I need to remind you of the luxuries provided to you?"

"No, my queen." I kept my eyes lowered. Even though Queen Math'ara wasn't present, she could see through the bugs' eyes. Despite her level tone, she was furious. If I got back to Valenmae with the king's head, the Aethrium Stone, and the Shadow Slinger in a cage yesterday, I would have been too late. When I returned home, I wasn't going to be showered with praise for doing the impossible. I'd be scolded for taking longer than she expected.

"Do I need to come there myself to ensure this happens?"

If I hadn't spent my entire life learning to control every little expression, the queen would have seen the stress her words evoked. If she showed up at Ethlow, more lives than the demon king's would be lost. She would slaughter everyone in her way, not caring about the innocent residents.

"Give me two weeks, and the job will be done." I didn't need that long, but I knew it was best to ask for more time than necessary.

"You have one week." She never gave me the time I asked for. Whether she knew I asked for more, expecting her to cut the time down, or if she knew what I was capable of, I wasn't sure. It was a little game we played.

"Yes, my queen."

"I expect a report as soon as Zathrian is dead. It's about time someone takes his throne. He doesn't deserve to be called a demon."

"Yes, my queen."

"Stop the groveling and stand up straight." Her orders were her way of reminding me she was always watching.

I straightened my back, keeping my face composed. I didn't speak again, knowing nothing I said mattered. It would have only served to upset the queen further.

"One week and not a second more. You are the Infernal Dagger of Valenmae, and I expect you to prove you deserve that title." I kept my mouth closed. "Do you understand?"

Stay silent. Speak. None of it mattered. No matter how many lives I took, no matter how many jobs I completed, it'd never be enough. As long as the signet was burned on my back, I didn't have a choice.

"Yes, my queen."

Queen Math'ara clicked her tongue, and the dragonflies scattered. My shoulders slumped, letting my exhaustion show. I couldn't move as the reminder of my deadline became set in stone.

I knew the queen was growing impatient, but there was only a week left on my timer, which meant there was no room for error.

Jasper chuffed, peeking his head out of the cave. He heard the entire conversation, but I had trained him well enough to know to stay far away whenever the queen was involved. The last thing I needed was for Queen Math'ara to learn of my secret attachment to my wyvern.

"Don't worry. This will all be over soon." I let my hand run over his head, and he nuzzled my chest. "Then we'll get to go home."

Chapter
15

I crouched on the top of the tallest tower of Ethlow, resisting the urge to pick at my clothes. It was the first version of the dragon scale armor I ever received. It pinched at my side and made it feel like I had a wedgie that was impossible to pick. I had been through torture and had learned to steal my mind. Most days, an uncomfortable outfit was something I could push through with ease, but I was restless.

The queen threatening to come to Ethlow herself unnerved me in a way I would never admit out loud, not even to Jasper. It shouldn't have bothered me. The residents of Ethlow didn't matter to me. In a matter of days, I would kill their king and let the place descend into chaos without those that kept it running. The estate would stay safe at night, since the king's magic was embedded into the walls. It had become a part of the building, growing into something beyond the king. It would continue to protect those inside.

Until it didn't.

Eventually, the strength of the underworld would grow beyond the protection of magic. Creatures would break through the doors and windows and feast on the unsuspecting if anyone dared to stay without their king.

Or maybe the creatures would go away without the demon king drawing them to this point in the mortal realm. They would go after the other four demon rulers left alive, until I was sent to kill them, too. I didn't know the likelihood of that. Queen Math'ara told me little about the creatures from the underworld, which meant she didn't understand them herself, or she didn't think I was worthy of that knowledge.

I watched the nightmares roaming the forest. They had been out for hours, and I studied them, learning their movements and patterns. One day, I'd be sent to defeat the creatures, and I had to understand them before that point. So I waited. I studied. I had taken down a couple of them in Valenmae, but Queen Math'ara liked to save my special abilities and send regular warriors to die instead.

"I'm surprised you had the arrogance to return to the estate after what you did." Viridian stood on a roof one level lower than me. He was more difficult to sense as shadows from the underworld danced with his own.

"I'm not in the mood tonight, Viridian."

It had been a matter of time before the paralytics wore off the demon. I had expected them to wear off sooner. Maybe they had, but he hadn't bothered to find me until now. That was unlikely. If he had done to me what I did to him, the first thing I would have done was return the favor with a knife of my own.

"And you think I'm in the mood? What part of this isn't a game don't you seem to understand?" The demon's usual filter was gone, his irritation flowing freely. Tonight, he wouldn't hold back from trying to kill me. I was sure of that.

I rose to my feet, feeling the ache in my legs after sitting in the same position for hours on end. I pulled out two daggers. "Let's get this over with."

Viridian tilted his head to the side a fraction of an inch. "I expected you to gloat and rub in your victory the moment I saw you."

"I thought you'd prefer this side of me." My voice was unusually dry. It was a tone I avoided using on everyone I met. I preferred others to see me as the wild assassin, because they took me less seriously. I didn't have the energy to think of witty banter designed to get under the Shadow Slinger's skin.

"Something happened."

I waited for the daggers to fly or the shadows to snap at my heels, initiating the fight. I had predicted the Shadow Slinger would have attacked me immediately after leaving him locked in the catacombs. Thirty seconds top. A full minute ticked by without incident.

Light danced across the sky, illuminating Viridian's teal eyes for a split second. Thunder quickly followed. The air smelled damp, and it was a matter of minutes before the clouds gave way.

"Aren't you supposed to demand I return the Aethrium Stone, threatening to kill me if I don't?" My fingers itched for a fight. The thrill always pushed the heaviness from my chest.

"Where is the Aethrium Stone?" The demon's voice lacked conviction. He only asked because I pushed him to.

"I'm not going to tell you that. You'll have to fight me to get that information." I tightened my grip on my daggers, prepared for him to slip into the shadows, only to reappear with a knife in my back.

Viridian didn't move. "Why are you eager for a fight?"

Irritation flared in my veins. The Shadow Slinger was supposed to attack the moment he saw me. I jumped down to the same level as him, landing lightly on my feet. "Why aren't you trying to kill me? I fucked you and then stabbed you, leaving you paralyzed on the disgusting prison floor."

The shadow demon took a few steps forward as he spoke, his hands clasped behind his back. "As I lay there unable to move, I thought about every way I could take my revenge. I thought about killing you slowly. I thought about killing you quickly. I thought about peeling your skin little by little. But then I thought about the last time someone had bested me so thoroughly, and you know what I concluded?"

This was different from every interaction I had had with the Shadow Slinger, and I didn't know what to make of it. "Humor me."

"You are the first to compromise me successfully."

The words should have brought me pleasure. Yesterday they would have.

"Does this mean you're in love with me, pretty boy?" My usual charm was missing, even in my attempt.

"Far from it, but it'd be a lie to say I didn't admire you." There was a glimmer in his eyes, but it wasn't from messing with me. The Shadow Slinger was being utterly honest.

Warmth bloomed in my chest, but sleet slipped from the sky. The icy rain cooled any moment of triumph that blossomed.

"Great. You admire me. It doesn't change the fact that we're enemies. So let's stop this chit chat and start trying to kill each other."

I let my dagger fly, aiming for the Shadow Slinger's shoulder. He twisted his torso, easily avoiding the attack, but I was already lunging for him. My blade scratched his cheek, and dark purple blood dribbled down the wound. He could have avoided my weapon with a single step backwards.

"Fight me," I growled.

"Tell me where you hid the Aethrium Stone, and I'll give you the fight of your life."

I slashed him again, this time slicing through his shirt. "Fight me, or I'll kill you."

Viridian stepped to the side, dodging my next attack. I was acting recklessly, but the thrum in my blood only grew stronger. I needed to fight to lessen the thundering inside my head, echoing the thunder in the sky.

"You might be good, but you're not that good. You couldn't kill me if you tried." Viridian smirked, taunting me.

He was wrong. If I wanted to kill him, I could have. He had been paralyzed, and I could have slit his throat and burned his body. If I wanted him dead, he would have been months ago.

"Fuck you," I growled.

"Are you that desperate to?" His eyes twinkled in an unusual light. He was the stone-faced, painfully serious Shadow Slinger. He wasn't the type to flirt and tease. He was the one I was able to rely on for a good fight, but he was failing me.

If he wasn't willing to fight me, I'd force him to. I screeched as I jumped at him. This time I aimed my dagger at his heart, anticipating his attempt to step to the side. It forced him to throw his arm up in defense. My dagger plunged into his arm. Using the dagger as an anchor, I flipped my body over him. I latched onto his back, wrapping my arm around his neck.

"Fight me!"

His fingers pushed between my arm and his throat, stopping me from crushing his windpipe. He could have slipped into the shadows, easily breaking free, but he didn't.

"No."

"Have you gone soft?" I didn't understand why the demon wouldn't fight me. Unless he physically couldn't. "Or are you still affected by the poison?"

"Tell me where the Aethrium Stone is, and I'll fight you." That was his second offer. He was trying to use my desperation against me, but it wasn't working. As much as I wanted to fight, giving up the Aethrium Stone was non-negotiable, especially when I left the artifact in Jasper's care.

"Fine. If you won't fight me, then I will fight your king." I released the shadow demon and took off at a run. It took exactly thirty-six steps to reach the end of that roof. I leapt to a lower level, but when I landed, my foot slid just enough to throw off my balance. The sleet made the roof tiles slick and unstable, but I didn't care.

The Shadow Slinger appeared in front of me, fury making his eyes glow. "Touch King Zathrian, and I'll have no choice but to kill you."

I dug my boots onto the roof, but they didn't have as much grip as the ones I was used to. I rolled to the side, my shoulders slamming on the tiles as I tumbled down. I dug my dagger into the tiles as I reached the edge of the estate, but the metal snapped in half. I twisted my body as I fell through the air, landing on my feet in the shape of a cat.

I shifted into human form, ready to take on the Shadow Slinger, but a putrid smell hit my nose, making me gag. I looked up at the ten-legged creature facing me with a mouth full of teeth, ready to devour me whole.

Chapter 16

I reached for the dagger strapped to my thigh, but it was scattered on the roof somewhere after chucking it at the shadow demon. The sheaths at my sides were also empty—one dagger had been embedded in Viridian's arm, the other had snapped on the roof. I didn't have my tenisium daggers with me. I was saving those for the demon king. That left me with two other weapons: one small blade in my boot, and one regular on my other leg. It wasn't much, but my body was a weapon.

The creature clicked its teeth, and then its body shivered. It wasn't cold. It was excited. I had five seconds to move before it slashed its razor legs through me. Icy calm washed over me in the face of danger. There was no room for error, which meant fun and frustration had no place in my mind.

I rushed forward, snatching my weapon from my thigh as I moved at an inhuman speed. I weaved between the creature's legs, swiping my dagger up in an attempt to split open its guts. The blade ripped through its skin, making it slough to the ground. Beneath the soft exterior, there was a hard exoskeleton that chipped the iron in my blade.

I should have kept one of the tenisium daggers on me at all times, but there was no use fretting over that. The creature slashed its back leg, but I dove out of the way, shifting in a wolf as I hit the ground. Mud covered my fur. The sleet was unrelenting, turning the ground into a sloshy mess. It gave little traction for movement, but I had trained in rain, snow, and a hurricane. Queen Math'ara had ensured I was prepared for anything, anywhere, anytime.

The creature jumped, swiping four legs at me all at once. I rushed to meet the attack, digging my sharpened canines into its leg. I thrashed my head, and the creature screamed as I ripped its leg clean off. As it attacked again, it lost another limb, and then another. When over half the legs were missing, the creature crashed to the ground.

I shifted back into human form, grabbing the dagger from my boot. I sank the blade into one of its eyes. Black blood squirted as I ripped it out and took out the rest of its sight. Before I finished off the monster, the air thickened. Other beasts were almost upon me, drawn closer by the dying scream of their fellow underworld dweller.

I shrank into the form of a rat, barely dodging the attack of a thing that resembled an enormous mutated bear with two heads and claws the length of my arm. It stomped on the ground, splashing muddied water and making it difficult to see. I leaped out of the way and shifted into crow form, but the mud weighed down my wings, making it impossible to fly. When I hit the ground again, I was a bear that was half the size of the creature in front of me. The larger the creature I transformed into, the more energy it took from my reserves. I could have matched the size of the beast, but I had to preserve my energy with the four other creatures breathing down my back.

I slashed one of the heads of the imposter bear, gouging an eye in the process. Black oozed from its face. As it tried to return the attack, I was already turning away to block the four-legged creature from biting my leg. I hit it away, and then shrank to an alligator. My body slid through the mud with ease, allowing me to snap my jaw around the middle of the beast. Its blood filled my mouth, making me gag from the putrid taste. I pushed through the physical response and crushed the four-legged creature between my teeth.

The beast slumped in my mouth, and I released it. A sharp pain erupted from my tail as the bear-like creature stepped on me. I shifted into a fox, freeing my body and dashing away. Two more ten legged creatures appeared from the forest, adding to the danger. I was outnumbered.

Part of being a skilled assassin was knowing when I was in over my head. I shifted into my human form and chucked my last dagger into the neck of the closest creature and took off running towards the estate. The forest wasn't an option with the other creatures lurking nearby. I jumped, grabbing the edge of the roof, and hoisted myself up.

A sharp pain erupted from my chest. I looked down, and there was a leg sticking out of my torso. My fingers dug into the roof, refusing to let the creature rip me off. I clicked my boots together, releasing a secret blade embedded in the sole of my shoe. I twisted, cutting off the leg piercing my body.

My fingers slipped off the roof as my strength gave out. I landed in a crouch and faced the creatures. I was outnumbered and out of weapons. I had been in a worse scenario. I couldn't think of it with the impending fight, but I knew it was true. A lot of mindless underworld creatures were not going to be the end of me.

Jasper needed me. Myst'elle was waiting for me to come home. Queen Math'ara would not accept my failure. She'd go to the underworld and drag my soul from the depths of the shadows to punish me if I died before she allowed it.

The creatures came at me. I screeched, ready to make my final stand against them. I would not die. Rushing forward, I slid through the mud. I twisted around their bodies as they attacked me. They hit each other as they missed me. Three went down, one after another, but it left another three angry and ready to destroy me.

I tried to shift again. If I pushed my body hard enough, I could sprout wings and get to safety. Pain pulsed from deep within. I was running on fumes. I pressed my hand against my side, trying to slow the bleeding. I barely felt the pain, my body too numb from the icy water raining down on me. Each breath grew more difficult, but I wasn't done.

There was a lattice on the other side of the estate near the kitchen. I could use that to climb up and make it to the roof. I'd have to contend with the Shadow Slinger there, but he wouldn't kill me. He had his chance to and chose not to. He was the safer option over the creatures.

I took off in a run, refusing to let my injuries slow my pace. I got three steps in before I sensed the attack. I tried to bend out of the way, but my body was moving slower than I was used to. Pain ripped through my calf as a ghastly leg pierced the muscles. I tumbled to the ground, twisting as I fell. The creature's leg snapped under my weight, freeing me enough to move. Another leg slammed down towards me, but my hand caught it before it hit anything vital. With a swift yank, the creature lost another leg. I tossed the limb to the side, ignoring the throb that came from the barbs embedded in my fingers. Another attack launched for me, and all I could do was roll out of the way.

The creatures surrounded me, and I was struggling to find a way out.

This was not the end.

I refused to be taken down like this.

I forced myself to my feet, but I stumbled, my body not wanting to cooperate.

I braced for the next attack, but shadows shot from the sky, surrounding me like a shield. The Shadow Slinger stepped out from them, a rapier in his hand.

"I'm assuming you know how to use this." Viridian shoved the weapon into my hand. I nodded. "Good. You better be ready."

I turned my back to him, holding the sword while digging my feet into the ground. Pain radiated through my body, but I used it to ground myself. Pain was either the death of a fighter or what set them apart from others.

The shields dropped, and Viridian and I launched into action. I slashed the uninjured face of the two-headed bear, quickly ramming the blade into its center. I cut off the second head, leaving no room for error. I turned to help Viridian, but shadows whipped towards the beasts, cracking like waves of thunder. The dark whips moved in flashes, almost too fast to see. Parts of the creatures flung away from their bodies until they were dismembered.

The monsters didn't have a chance to touch Viridian, and it became evidently clear how he received the name "Shadow Slinger."

Between the two of us, the battle ended in seconds.

The shadow demon turned to me, his hair plastered to his face from the unrelenting sleet. "You got the fight you demanded after all."

I stared at the demon, my breath ragged. He didn't have to intervene. If he had left me to fend for myself, there was a 95 percent chance the creatures would have taken care of me—taken care of his problem.

"Why did you step in like that?" My voice was barely audible over the freezing weather.

"These creatures threaten Ethlow."

I shook my head. It wasn't a real answer. Both of us knew it. "Why did you come to my aid?" Out of every calculation and prediction I had made, the Shadow Slinger's help had never come to mind. I was his enemy, one he wanted dead—at least he should have if he was smart, and he *was* smart. It didn't make sense.

We stared at each other in unspoken silence. He knew as well as I did that there was no logical reason for him to step in.

"You stole the Aethrium Stone, and without your knowledge, I won't be able to find it." It was the closest thing to a lie he had ever spouted. He was more than capable of learning where I had been making camp. It could take time, but he'd find it with or without me. "We should go. More of those creatures will be on us in less than a minute."

Lightning illuminated the sky. There was something foreign written on his face—something I didn't understand.

"Right," I agreed. I took a step towards the estate, but my body remembered my injuries and the pain all at once. My legs gave out, unable to maintain my balance with my ripped muscles. I clutched my side, trying to hold the wound from bleeding out. If I had been a human, I would have been long dead, but my enhanced healing was the only thing keeping me alive as my body tried to shut down.

"Shapeshifter?" Viridian's voice sounded distant. "Shapeshifter."

I had lost too much blood, and my body couldn't keep up with it. The edges of my vision turned black. There was a 75 percent chance I was going to die. 50 if I managed to wrap my chest wound.

I tried to stand. I had to push through for a little longer. My arms gave out, and the rest of my vision turned dark.

"Kestria!"

Chapter 17

I couldn't bring myself to open my eyes. Everything was dark, and if I allowed myself into full consciousness, there was a chance I'd be in the underworld. Each breath was a struggle. My right lung barely wanted to work, and my left lung struggled to compensate. It would have been easy to fall back asleep, but I didn't know where I was or if I was safe.

I wiggled my toes and then my fingers. I wasn't paralyzed. I cracked my eyes open, and all I saw was black. My eyelids were too heavy to keep open. I focused on my breath and the pain. Pain meant I was alive. How, I didn't know.

Everything was cold. It was as if my bones had been frozen, so despite the warmth of my skin, there was a chill I couldn't shake. It only added to the heaviness of my body.

It was impossible to tell how much time had passed with my mind trapped in the darkness. The only solace was I was too tired to think, likely falling in and out of consciousness. A warm towel dabbed my forehead, pulling me into an alert state. I kept my eyes closed, listening for information about where I was.

"There's no point in pretending to be asleep." Viridian's voice came from my right as the warm cloth pulled away.

I didn't respond, challenging his statement. If I stayed silent, there was a chance he would think he was mistaken.

A low laugh responded to my silence, and my eyes snapped open. Teal eyes met mine, and I was quickly reminded of how difficult it was to breathe.

"I don't think I've ever heard you laugh. Didn't think it was possible, pretty boy." Speaking hurt, but I refused to show the struggle.

Viridian's lip twitched, as if he was resisting a smile. "The drugs must be making you hallucinate."

"Is that a lie from the faithful master of the house?" It was easy to fall back into banter with the shadow demon. My body was heavy, but my heart felt lighter. The Shadow Slinger had come to my aid. No one had done that for me before.

"You must be mistaken. I don't lie." The glint in his eyes made me question that.

I pushed myself up, and the demon's hand was on my back a second later, guiding me into a sitting position.

"You should rest."

"How can I rest in the presence of my enemy?"

Silence hung in the air. Enemies didn't save the other, dress their wounds, and bring them back to their bed. Waking up in the underworld would have made more sense than this.

"How long have I been out?" I asked when it was clear he wasn't going to answer.

"Three days."

I cursed internally. Time was running out, and there was too much to do. "I need to go." I lurched forward, ready to run out of the room, but a wave of dizziness washed over me.

Viridian grabbed my shoulders, steadying me. "You are too injured to go anywhere."

I had days before Queen Math'ara arrived at Ethlow and caused more mayhem than I would. "You don't understand. I don't have a choice."

"There is always a choice."

"Maybe when you work for kings like yours. I must go." I tried to get up, but the demon tightened his grip, refusing to let me move.

"You are in no state to leave."

"You don't understand."

"Return the Aethrium Stone." His voice was soft, boarding on a plea, but the Shadow Slinger wasn't the type to beg for anything. I stopped fighting him. The confusion and pain were disorienting, and I needed to sort through my thoughts.

I avoided his eyes. He already knew his suggestion wasn't a possibility. "Have you ever thought about adding some color to these walls? It's bland in here, but a colorful painting would make it look better." My voice cracked on the last word.

Viridian held a cup to my lips. "Drink." He lifted it slowly.

I coughed as a potent liquid hit my tongue. "That's disgusting."

"You nearly died. Drink."

"What if you're trying to poison me?" I scrunched my nose at the greenish liquid.

"I wrapped your wounds and prevented you from bleeding out, but yes, I plan to poison you." He lifted his brows, his voice dry.

"Was that a joke, pretty boy?"

He didn't respond, his eyes digging into me. His face said enough. Either I drank the disgusting liquid, or he wouldn't say another word. I sighed, knowing there was no winning this battle. I reached for the cup, wincing as the motion pulled at the healing wound in my chest. Viridian took over, helping me drink until every drop was gone.

He set the cup on the side table and stood. "You're in a better mood. I didn't realize nearly dying was the key." He faced away from me as he spoke, but I couldn't tear my eyes away, watching his every movement. His tail worked with his hands as he shuffled things on a tray on a small table. His hands were large and skilled—in more ways than one.

"Sometimes a good beating is what one needs." When my emotions built into unbearable levels, a good fight always cleared my head.

He looked at me briefly, the only signs of concern before returning to whatever he was doing.

"Why am I alive?" I asked. Years of training allowed me to keep my heart steady. Enemies could sense an erratic heartbeat, giving away signs of worry or anxiety. It was a weakness.

"Because I still have my uses for you."

"What kind of uses?"

The demon didn't respond, which only made my mind go to dangerous places. Places I didn't have time to go with Math'ara breathing down my neck.

"Am I your prisoner?" I asked, the silence too much to bear.

"Do you know how to stop talking?"

I huffed a laugh and then immediately grunted from the pain in my side. I had had plenty of broken bones and deep cuts but never a damaged lung.

Viridian was by my side a second later, his hand on my back. His eyes flared, and if I didn't know better, I would have thought he was concerned about me. "You should rest. If you're not careful, you will tear open your stitches and bleed all over my bed."

I wanted to ask him why he cared about my health, but even if I had the bravery needed to ask a dangerous question like that, there was only a five percent chance he would answer.

"Why did you agree to serve King Zathrian when you are more powerful than him?" I decided to stick with a safer topic.

Viridian didn't respond, but he also didn't move. I was painfully aware of the way his hand lingered on my bare skin. My torso was only covered in bandages, leaving me more exposed than I liked.

"Because the sire has a heart more pure than non-demons. He believes the world is good, even in the face of evil. If the mortal realm has a chance to become something brighter, he is the key."

"If you believe in good, then why not take control of a kingdom? You could do more by ruling than by following."

"I do not have pure intentions like the sire." There was no shame in his statement. To him, it was a fact.

"But you want the world he is imagining. Doesn't that make you good?"

"I would not use the same methods as him. Therefore, any good that is accomplished would not result in a better world. It is best that my powers stay in check, and Zathrian is the only one I trust enough to ensure that happens."

I struggled to understand where he was coming from. "If I had a choice between freedom or doing good for the world, I would choose freedom."

"Then why don't you?"

I huffed, ignoring the ache in my ribs. "It's not that simple, pretty boy. If you asked your king for freedom, he would give it to you. If I asked my queen the same thing, she would break every bone in my body to ensure I never had the audacity to ask for it again. That is why you would have been better off letting me die. We will always be enemies, and nothing will change that."

Shadows danced along Viridian's shoulder's, but his face was unreadable. "Give King Zathrian the Aethrium Stone and ask him for help. He will protect you."

His words were a scheme and not a genuine offer. It was impossible that he offered sanctuary to me with sincerity. It was a manipulation tactic to get me to reveal where I had hid the ancient artifact—one I would have used myself.

"And bring war to Kinzlea, to Ethlow? No thanks. Besides, I don't need anyone to protect me. I have been taking care of myself my entire life. You should see my place in Valenmae. I have an enormous room with the biggest bed. I have everything I could ever want there. You should see it sometime."

Viridian studied me, making me feel too exposed. I didn't like it. I had spent years learning to craft my life into the perfect facade, all to be the perfect weapon for my queen. If Viridian continued looking at me like that, he'd break down my walls, one brick at a time.

"Maybe one day I will." His response threw me off. He wasn't supposed to accept it like it was a real possibility.

The conversation was getting dangerous. "I'm starving. If I don't eat some of your delicious cooking soon, I might actually die." I gave my best pleading look to the demon.

He let out a long sigh and stood. "For a prisoner, you are very demanding."

"I'm your prisoner?" I smirked at him, loving his irritation. "Because you took me to bed instead of a prison cell, and I don't see any shackles."

"Don't get used to it, Kestria."

My comeback got lost in my throat as he used my name. It felt too personal, and I didn't like it. The Shadow Slinger was my enemy. I needed him to hate me, because it would be easier to kill his king and betray his trust—not that I had a choice. It was either my life or his, and I would always choose my life.

Viridian stepped into the shadows, disappearing from sight.

I stood the second his shadows dissipated. My head spun, and my body protested. I was in no condition to continue. I needed at least two more days to fully recover from injuries this severe, but

I didn't have two days. There was too much to do to stop Queen Math'ara from taking over my carefully laid out plan.

Both of my dragon scale armor suits were folded and set out on a bench below the window, as if the Shadow Slinger was prepared to call a truce between us. I grabbed the armor and hurried out of the room. I needed to be long gone before he came back and threw me into the dungeon. Or before he tried to convince me to change sides.

No matter what strange kindness he showed me, we would always be enemies, and there was no path I could take that would ever change that.

Chapter
18

Not being able to shapeshift was inconvenient. Human legs were slow compared to other forms, and every second I wasted put me at risk for Viridian coming after me. I had to put the final pieces together before I was out of time. There was one mind left that I had to convince before telling Elcy it was time to execute the plan.

The library was empty, which wasn't unusual. Walking through the bookshelves on human legs was exhausting, especially with the injury in my calf.

A flare of magic erupted in the room before two voices hit my ears. "That makes no sense."

"It's better than your theory."

I climbed onto the nearest bookshelf, ignoring the splitting pain in my body. I had been through worse training with similar injuries. It was essential for an assassin to function when injured. Queen Math'ara had wounded me on countless occasions to make sure I thrived under any condition. It made me a better assassin.

"I think it's completely possible that Viridian finally fucked Zathrian. He's like a loyal puppy."

My ears perked at the mention of Viridian on the librarian's tongue.

"There is no way. Zathrian is loyal to that human. Besides, it's impossible for Viridian to be gay. If he was, he would have picked me over Zathrian. I'm much hotter." The king of Mithcourt said the statement with full chest.

"You're such an arrogant asshole," the librarian grumbled. "You're only hotter because of your flames."

"Yet you chose to fuck me instead."

"Yeah, and I'm forgetting why right now."

"Let me remind you."

The librarian squeaked, and I didn't have to see the pair to know exactly what they were doing. There was no choice but to wait it out, since it wasn't as easy to sneak around in human form, and I needed to speak to the witch before Viridian came looking for me and dragged me back to bed. I couldn't afford the delay, and I couldn't explain to him the seriousness of needing to leave.

I shook my head, realizing that train of thought was ridiculous. The Shadow Slinger wouldn't have dragged me back to his bed to ensure a proper recovery. He had only saved me to make it easier to retrieve the Aethrium Stone.

"You can't distract me that easily," the witch said after a long minute. "I'm serious. Viridian is acting strangely. I don't think I've ever seen him act so moody one day, then smile the next. Something is going on, and you need to ask Zathrian about it."

"Or I could bend you over and fuck you right here."

The witch hesitated, taking a moment to consider his offer. "Talk to Zathrian. Don't make me ask you again."

A rush of heat rolled over the library, and then the witch let out a long sigh. I waited from on top of the bookshelf. When the librarian walked by, I jumped down, landing in front of her.

She screamed, grabbing her chest. "What is your problem? You can't scare people like that. You made me pee myself a little."

I tried to bite back my smile, but I couldn't. "You're funny."

"How is peeing myself funny?"

I shrugged, delighting in her pain a little too much. "It just is."

Her face tightened, making her cheeks look extra puffy. Between her big brown eyes and short, round stature, she looked like an adorable doll dress in black. "Who are you, anyway?"

I placed my hand on my chest and gasped. "You don't recognize me? After everything I've done for you?"

Her eyes narrowed as she searched her memories, but she had never met me in regular form. "Of course, I remember you."

I leaned in a little, and she bent backwards to put distance between us. "Then what's my name?"

The witch stepped to the side, unable to hide the strangled noise of her distress. "I forgot. I'm bad with names. And people." She gathered a handful of books that had been scattered on tables and placed them on a cart.

"Let me reintroduce myself, then. I am the wonderful and incredibly amazing Kestria."

The librarian tensed. She emptied her hands before turning slowly. "You're Kestria?"

"That's what I said, isn't it?"

The witch clicked her tongue. "I know. I heard you."

"Then why did you question it?"

The librarian's magic surged as her irritation grew. "I could call King Jathral back right now and have him tell Zathrian everything about you."

I smirked at the witch's audacity. She was brave for someone who could barely breathe regularly. "You won't do that because you owe me a life debt, and you don't like to owe anyone anything. That's also why you won't call your boy toy back here. Why have him do your dirty work when you are too independent to need him? How did you manage to break the king of Mithcourt, anyway?"

The witch struggled to sort through my words. She knew every one of them was true, but she'd never admit it out loud. "What do you want, and it better be good, because life debt or not, if you are here to hurt me or anyone else I care about, I won't hesitate to destroy you."

I grinned at her claim. She was a strong witch, but she overestimated her abilities. She wouldn't have been able to take me out, even in my injured state. "You already know what I want. Elcy told you."

"I want to hear it from your mouth."

I was prepared for the librarian to be the toughest one to convince. She was used to being alone, and she was more critical than the others.

I moved to the closest chair and sank into it. Each movement hurt, but sitting was a small reprieve. "I can't do this without you. I need all five of you to agree, but more than that, I need your magic. Elcy told you why I need your help. I'm trapped under Queen Math'ara's signet. You know better than the others that the five demon rulers are no joke. I won't be able to trap her and force her to remove her mark without your help. Without your magic."

The witch pulled at her fingers, looking down at the table. "Are you sure this is the only way?"

She was close, but she needed a push. I had anticipated that appealing to her emotions wasn't going to be enough. I had another trick up my sleeve, but I wanted to hold off a moment longer. "I don't like asking for help. If I had any other choice, I wouldn't be here."

She licked her lips, struggling to get past her final hesitation. "I'm not convinced. You're an assassin. You kill people."

"That is the definition of an assassin." I placed my feet on the table, spreading my legs in a V-shape. Elevating my leg helped with the throbbing, but I wanted it to look like a power play.

"Your sass isn't appreciated. You want my help. Give me a real reason." The librarian crossed her arms together, pushing her plush chest together in the process.

I grabbed my bag of rings from my pocket and tossed it on the table. The leather clattered against the wood with the rings clinking together.

"Do you know what that is?" I asked.

The witch reached forward, her eyes narrowed. I snatched the bag before she could grab it. The rings were a lifeline I couldn't risk.

"I sense magic," the witch said slowly.

"I know an artisan who crafts magic imbued items. She mostly deals with weapons, but for me, she makes rings. Each one does something a little different." I plucked a thin, silver-banded ring with an opal circle on it. "This one allows you to teleport small objects a short distance." I slipped it on and lifted my arm. A book that had been left on the table appeared in my hand in the blink of an eye.

The witch's eyes sparkled. She was hooked. "What else can your rings do?"

"Whatever I ask for. The artisan is the most skilled witch and crafter I know." It wasn't exactly true. Several requests had been denied over the years, because they were "too ridiculous," but it didn't stop me from pushing boundaries.

The librarian's eye twitched. "I'd like to meet this skilled witch sometime." She felt challenged.

I dug into the bag until I found a simple obsidian ring. I pressed my nail into a small divot, which created a split in space. I reached my hand through and pulled out a small leather-bound book. "I thought you might be interested in this information." I waved it in front of her face. "This contains notes from the artificer."

Tareen reached for the book, but I pulled it back.

"Help me, and I'll give you this."

The witch's eyes widened as she focused on the book. She was practically drooling over it. "What kind of notes?"

I flipped through the pages, taking my time. "Oh, just details on experiments. What worked. What didn't. That kind of thing. I don't have any interest in it, so I was thinking of throwing it out to save space."

Tareen's body lurched forward. "I'd kill you if you threw out such valuable information."

I would never throw out the artificer's notes. She was already going to kill me for stealing from her. "If you're willing to make a deal, I suppose I can give it to you instead."

Tareen tapped her fingers against the table. "Throw in a ring, and you have a deal."

I held out my hand, grinning with success. "You have yourself a deal." Tareen took my hand, and I shook my arm wildly. "It's been a pleasure, witch."

I needed to make one last stop before heading back to the cave to make the final preparations for my trap. Residents didn't think twice as they passed me. The beings living at Ethlow liked to keep to themselves, so they didn't know everyone, despite living at the estate for years. A little confidence and a touch of swagger, and I blended in with ease.

I kept my eyes on the shadows, waiting for them to move in a way I had become a little too familiar with, but they never did.

When I made it to the pixie's room, I didn't bother to knock as I burst through the door. The pixie was locked in an embrace with her pirate lover, but the moment she saw me, she pulled away, and her pixie dust brightened.

"Have you ever heard of knocking?"

I brushed her off. "Friends don't knock."

"Do you know this redhead?" The pirate looked me up and down.

Elcy's eyes widened, panic filling her face. She kept my secret from him, which was a surprise. "She's my friend. Can we have a minute alone?"

The captain's face tightened. Either he didn't believe her, or he didn't trust me. "Fine, but I'll be right outside if you need anything."

"Don't worry, Captain Booty, I'll take precious care of your pixie." *Unlike you.* I kept the comment to myself. If I insulted him, it'd be harder to get him to leave.

"We'll be quick," Elcy promised.

With a grumble, the captain left the room.

"He's awfully protective of you after everything that happened," I said. When I first met the pixie, she and the captain weren't lovers. After his betrayal, I had expected her to put her feelings aside and move on. I would have if I had been in her situation.

"He's changed."

"People don't change that easily."

Elcy pursed her lips. "Why are you here?"

"Straight to business. I like you." I sat on her bed, stretching out and getting comfortable. "I have excellent news. I have done what you failed to do and convinced the others to help. In three days, it will be time to take action."

"Three days?" Elcy gulped.

It gave me an extra day to return to Valenmae before Queen Math'ara's patience ran out, as well as time to fully recover. To take on the Shadow Slinger and the demon king, I needed to be in nothing less than perfect condition. "Three days and you get to go on your grand adventure with Captain Booty. Now listen closely because if everything doesn't go according to plan, things will go very wrong. I need you to tell the others to meet me in the greenhouse at noon on the planned day."

"Why the greenhouse?" Elcy asked.

"Because to face darkness, I need a place of light." It was the perfect cheesy response to the pixie. She wouldn't question my choice further. The greenhouse was the perfect place to keep unnecessary bystanders and the king away while I captured Viridian.

Chapter 19

J asper nuzzled me awake. I had lost track of how long I had slept
for. My body was stiff, but the pain from the attack was gone.
Jasper pushed at my side again, as if he was worried about me. I
rubbed his head, and he chuffed in response.

"I'm getting up." I stretched my limbs, forcing the exhaustion
away. Tomorrow was the day everything was to go down. With
Elcy's help, the plan was ready. Now, I needed everyone to show
up at the right place and time.

Jasper shoved me again, digging his nose beneath my back.
"Jasper. Give me a moment."

"The beast is trying to warn you that you've been caught slack-
ing." The female voice had me on my feet in a second flat.

Queen Math'ara stepped out of the shadows. Four horns
emerged from her head, two small ones at the front, and two twice
the size behind them. Her brown hair was pulled into intricate
braids around her horns. She stood tall, easily looking down at
me with her heels adding to her impressive height. Her lips were
painted a soft pink, but her eyes had dark coal smudged around
the edges, deepening the gray-blue within.

"Queen Math'ara." I bowed, showing the respect she expected.

"No wonder you are taking this long to complete your task if you are lazing around like this." She turned to Jasper and motioned for him to go to her with a pointed claw.

I couldn't breathe as her attention shifted to him. He glanced at me for permission—the worst thing he could have done. I gave him a subtle nod, and he plodded forward.

Queen Math'ara stroked under his chin. "A loyal beast you have here."

I didn't answer. She was testing me, and if she learned how much my wyvern meant to me... I refused to think about what would happen.

"I'm exhausted from the trip here, and imagine my surprise when I find you sleeping on the job." The threat was clear in her voice. She was unhappy with me and was deciding what to do.

"Everything is in order for my plan. By sunset tomorrow, the king of Kinzlea will be dead, and you will have the Shadow Slinger trapped and at your mercy." If I reassured her I was ready to strike, maybe I could stop the queen from unleashing her horrors on Ethlow.

"Why not tonight? Do you have to catch up on sleep?"

I could tell her I had been gravely injured and needed the rest to ensure I was at full strength, but it would have only hurt my case. Queen Math'ara was void of empathy. She thrived on other's pain and left no room for excuses.

"There are a lot of moving parts. In order to ensure I complete all three tasks set before me, it took careful planning."

The queen pulled her hand away from Jasper, but I didn't dare acknowledge him. With her around, I couldn't afford to say good-bye to him when I left for Ethlow. He knew the plan. If I didn't return home, he was to leave. If there was a way for me to tell him to leave tonight, I would have. I wanted him as far away from the queen as possible.

"Nine months of planning is unlike you, my little Infernal Dagger. If I didn't know any better, I would have guessed you took as long as you did to avoid coming home. To avoid me."

"Never, my queen." I held her eyes, letting her see the confidence in my statement. Crafting the emotions of my face and steeling my body was essential to play the part of assassin, spymaster, and thief. It made it easy to blend in, and it prevented the queen from reading my thoughts.

"No, you wouldn't dare. You've been trained better than that." The doubt in her voice made my muscles tighten. How would she test my loyalty after this was all over?

Jasper couldn't return home with me. It was too dangerous. When this was all done, I'd say goodbye and send him away forever. It was too risky for him to be associated with me. The queen had caught a whiff of his love, which was more than enough. Friends and loved ones were too dangerous to have. Myst'elle was my only safe friend. As the queen's daughter, she was immune to the queen's torture. Queen Math'ara loved her daughter in her own twisted way. She coddled the princess and showed her a side no one else was privy to. There was only a .5 percent chance the queen would harm her daughter to control me.

"Maybe I should go to the demon king's estate tonight to ensure you don't fail me." She glanced at her nails, acting as if she had decided to visit a neighbor.

"No!" The protest came out too quickly, and I had to recover. "If you go to Ethlow tonight, it will put King Zathrian on edge. I have everything in place for tomorrow. I will succeed, and you will have the king's head soon."

"And what of the Aethrium Stone?"

"I have located that as well. Everything you asked of me will come to fruition tomorrow." Confidence was the key to dealing with the queen, but I had to walk a fine line. She didn't take well to begging, but if I acted as if I knew better than her, it was worse.

"Fine, but I expect you to retrieve the Aethrium Stone tonight. I will not put up with incompetence. Understood?"

I bowed in respect. "Yes, my queen."

"Then go."

I flew as fast as I could to Ethlow, hardly able to breathe as I raced the sun—but it had nothing to do with physical exertion. Queen Math'ara was in Kinzlea, and she was with Jasper. She gave me a week, but I should have known that meant less time. If I was on time, I was late. I shouldn't have given myself days to recover, but if I hadn't, then I wouldn't have been at full strength for tomorrow.

I shouldn't have tried to get Viridian to fight me. The moment Queen Math'ara sent those dragonflies, I should have sped up my plan. It was best I returned to Valenmae as soon as possible. The sweet-natured and naïve residents made me soft, and I couldn't afford that.

As I reached the balcony on the far side of the estate, I transformed into a human. I slipped through the window as the setting sun invited creatures of the underworld to breach the world. I shut the window behind me and took in the scent of leather and antiseptic.

It was the last place I should've been, especially with the queen breathing down my back, but it was the one place I wanted to be. The room was void of the demon, but the sound of running water echoed from the conjoining room.

I burst into the washroom without a thought. Viridian stood below steaming water, letting it run over his naked body. Beads of water ran down the dips and curves of his sculpted back all the way to his tail, but my eyes focused on the mark between his shoulder blades. Black ink formed the shape of two horns that overlapped one another in the center. It stretched from shoulder to shoulder and radiated power.

The signet of the demon king of Kinzlea.

"Do you have any sense of privacy?" Viridian didn't look at me as he ran his fingers through his soapy hair.

"You saw me completely naked, so I figured it was fair to see you the same." My breathing quickened, unable to control my pulse as I took in every part of his exposed body. He had been inside of me, but I had never seen so much of him. It was a glorious sight and the perfect distraction.

Viridian took his time rinsing off before turning to me, revealing the rest of his body. He wasn't the bulky kind of muscular that the demon king was. The Shadow Slinger's muscles were toned to lethal and lithe levels. It was perfection, and it made me want one thing.

"Are you going to continue to ogle me, or are you going to hand me a towel?" He quirked an eyebrow, and it made my heart stutter.

I grabbed the perfectly folded towel and lifted it. He reached for it, but I dropped it on the floor. "Oops."

He huffed. "The audacity you have never ceases to amaze me."

I gestured in a dramatic bow. "Thank you. It comes naturally."

Viridian's horns fluttered as his eyes darkened. He stepped out of the tub and reached for the towel. I stepped on it and kicked it away.

"Are you trying to start a fight?" His voice came out as a low growl. He no longer found my actions funny, which only excited me.

"You have two choices." I lifted my pointer finger. "You can either fight me."

"Or?"

I lifted a second finger. "Or you can fuck me."

"And what if I wish to do neither?"

I looked down before meeting his eyes again. "Your body says otherwise."

A snarl erupted from his mouth, and he was on me a second later.

Chapter
20

Viridian wrapped his hand around my throat and pinned me against the wall. "Do you think you can interrupt my shower and make demands of me?" His eyes burned into mine, and I knew I had won.

"Looks like it." I winked at him, adding fuel to the fire. I didn't care which way this went, but the angrier he got, the better.

"You are infuriating."

"Yet you keep putting up with me. If I didn't know better, I'd say you like me." My skin was on fire as Viridian held my neck. It was hard enough to keep me pinned, but it barely restricted the air flow.

"You stabbed me." Viridian's hands ran down my side before removing both daggers strapped to my ribs.

"You liked it." I arched my body, desperate for his touch. I needed to stop thinking for a few minutes, and there were only two times my mind went blank: fucking or fighting. I didn't know which one I wanted more. Either. Both. I didn't care, as long as the demon holding my life in his hands made my brain stop for a few minutes.

Viridian pressed his mouth against my neck and bit down, his sharp teeth piercing my skin. I groaned at the sensation, digging my nails into the back of his neck. He plucked a third dagger off my body and chucked it. It thunked into the wall as he sucked on my neck, running his tongue over the pierce marks he had made.

"You're not going to trick me again, shapeshifter." He pressed his firm body against mine. His knee pushed my legs apart, settling between them. I rolled my hips, desperate for the friction.

"No tricks tonight, Viridian." His name on my tongue tasted delicious.

"And you expect me to believe you?" He snatched two more daggers off my body and tossed them somewhere I'd worry about later.

"No." I reached down and wrapped my fingers around his cock, earning a grunt as he thrusted into my touch. "But I expect you to fuck me, anyway."

Viridian grabbed my wrists and pinned them both above my head with a single hand. His tail ran over my inner thighs, making my body tighten as the twin tips moved dangerously close to my core. He plucked another dagger off as his tail slid over my pants, creating friction. He pulled away before giving me what I wanted.

I growled, and he grabbed my jaw, forcing me to look at him.

"You need to learn patience."

My chest heaved, feeling raw. Even in the prison cell, I had kept my guard up, constantly thinking about how to get out of the situation and manipulate the Shadow Slinger. This time was different. Queen Math'ara was breathing down my neck, ready to destroy the estate and me if I didn't complete my tasks.

There was only one last thing to do to ensure tomorrow went off without a hitch, but that could happen later. Tonight was my last night of freedom for a while, and there was only one thing I truly wanted to do with it.

"I have no interest in being patient. I have no interest in thinking, so are you going to fuck me, or should I find someone else to do the job?"

Shadows erupted from the demon, blocking out any light in the room. I couldn't see anything, but I felt his breath in my ear.

"If anyone else touches you, they die. Understood?"

My pulse thrummed in my head, unable to consider what his words meant. Whatever he felt towards me, whatever I felt towards him, it didn't matter, because tomorrow I would betray him, and his hatred for me would spiral into the underworld.

"If you don't want someone else to do the job, then you better do it yourself," I taunted.

Hands and shadows roamed my body, removing my clothes piece by piece. I couldn't predict where he would touch me next, which heightened my senses. His tail slid through the slickness between my legs. One tip flicked my clit while the other teased my entrance.

"You are insufferable." Viridian nipped above my collarbone. "Maddening." His teeth grazed my breast. "Psychotic." His lips ghosted over my navel. "Devastating." He nuzzled his face between my legs, and his mouth found the apex of my thighs. "And I can't stop thinking about destroying you." He hooked his shoulder beneath my leg, lifting it up to give him a better angle to dive deeper.

His tongue moved skillfully between my clit and my entrance. I grabbed his wet hair, needing something to hold onto. I let my head fall back as every thought left my brain. All that mattered was that moment and the way the demon's tongue coaxed pleasure from me. The pressure started at my core, but as he continued devouring me as if it was his last meal, it spread all over my body until it released like a wave crashing onto the shore. I cried out, gripping his hair harder as white fire burned through my soul.

Viridian didn't stop until he lapped up every last drop of me. He lowered my leg back to the ground, but I felt unsteady. My body shook, but I didn't want it to end. I pulled the demon to his feet and grabbed the back of his head.

"You're not done, are you?" I nipped his bottom lip, hungry for a taste of him.

"Far from it." Viridian grabbed my ass, his claws piercing the skin as he lifted me up.

I wrapped my legs around him, and his cock plunged into my entrance. Each time he slammed into me, he pressed me against the wall. His motions were sharp, fast, and unrelenting. I dug my nails into his neck, drawing blood. His growl only fed my pleasure. I wanted to hear him come undone, knowing it was all because of me.

He carried me out of the washroom and moved straight for his bed. He pulled me off him, and I immediately reached for his cock, needing any kind of physical contact to force my thoughts away.

His tail wrapped around my wrist, pulling my hand away. Viridian grabbed my chin and lowered his face to mine. "You want me to fuck you, and that's exactly what I will do, but I'm in control." There was no room for argument in his tone, but it only made me want to challenge him.

"Are you sure your stamina can keep up with me?" I smirked, knowing exactly how much that comment burrowed under his skin.

Viridian picked me up and flipped me around, so I was on my hands and knees. His hand pressed on my lower back, forcing me to arch for him. *Smack!* The sting on my bottom wasn't from his hands, both of which were holding me still. His twin tipped tail made my skin sting in two lines.

"Want to try that again?" His voice was a low growl that went straight between my legs. Any other person would have given up control from the threat alone, but I wanted more.

"You're ancient compared to me. I could easily outlast you."
Smack!

His lips brushed against the sting, leaving soft whispers in his wake. "I'll give you one more chance to beg properly, or I will tie you up and leave you for the rest of the night." He bit into my ass as a threat and a promise.

My breath stopped in my throat as my desire and need to fight back battled one another.

"I'm going to need you to speak, Kestria." He kissed lower, skirting around the one area I wanted most. I arched my back harder, trying to move his face between my legs, but his fingers dug into my hips, refusing to give me what I wanted. "I need words."

"Please." The word escaped my mouth without a thought. For once, the demon won the battle, my desperation for release too great.

"That's a good girl." He slammed into me with all his strength before I had a chance to respond. His thrusts were sharp and powerful. His fingers gripped my hips, his need flowing through the strength of his hands. He wanted this as much as me. For a moment, we weren't enemies. We didn't work for opposing rulers. I wasn't here to kill his king.

For a moment, it was the two of us, finding pleasure in ways others had never reached before. In his shadows, I wasn't an assassin, lurking in darkness, ready to kill. I was simply me. No more. No less.

When his grunts became more frequent, he grabbed my hair and pulled me flushed against his torso. His tail reached around and rubbed my clit. The pain from my hair being pulled mixed with his cock sliding in and out of me while his tail stroked my bundle of nerves pushed me over the edge. I cried out as my walls pulsed around him. His pace didn't slow until one final thrust.

Viridian pulled out of me and released me, letting me tumble onto his bed. His warm seed spewed on my backside in triumph, and I couldn't move. I slumped the rest of the way, focusing on my breath. Viridian stepped away, but I couldn't bring myself to see where he went. A moment later, a warm washcloth wiped over my body.

I pushed myself up and studied the demon's face in the dark. "What are you doing?" With others, it had never been like that. Once the sex was over, we parted our ways, our needs met.

"Cleaning you up."

"Why?"

"You're talking a lot."

I pressed my lips together, unable to process what was happening. I rolled over, knowing I needed to leave. "I should go."

Viridian was on top of me in a split second, pinning me to his bed. "I'm not done with you yet. You're going to regret questioning my stamina." His lips met mine, desperate and hungry, and my body went limp.

I should have left. Tomorrow, I would destroy his entire world. He'd look back at tonight and think it was another ploy. It was better that way, because the truth would only hurt.

My body was heavy as I lay in Viridian's bed, unable to move. Neither of us had spoken since the last round, and I lost track of time long ago. Every part of me was exhausted, except my mind. Tonight was not a night for sleep. Instead, I watched Viridian's chest move up and down in a steady rhythm.

He wasn't asleep anymore than I was, but there were no words to describe what had just happened.

"Whatever you're planning tomorrow, don't go through with it." Viridian's voice was barely audible.

I put on my mask, crafting my body into the perfect image. I wasn't surprised he had learned I was up to something. He was a master of shadows and knew everything that went on within the estate. The problem came if he knew too much.

"I'm not planning anything tomorrow."

Viridian rolled over and grabbed my jaw. "At least half of what comes out of this mouth is a lie." His thumb brushed over my lower lip, and desire flashed in his eyes. His hand dropped a moment later.

"If you think I'm planning something, then why am I lying here, uninjured and unrestrained?" The demon had had plenty of opportunities to take me down, yet he chose not to repeatedly. It made no sense. I kept him alive because that was what Queen Math'ara wanted. If she wanted him dead, he wouldn't have been lying next to me.

Viridian didn't respond. Either he didn't want to, or he didn't know the answer himself. "Why do you follow Queen Math'ara?"

"Why do you follow King Zathrian?"

"You're deflecting."

I tried to roll away, ready to leave, but Viridian caught my arm, pulling me into his chest. It would have been easy to get out of his grasp.

"Kestria."

My name on his tongue made my chest tighten. "You know my origin story. I wasn't given any other choice but to make a deal with the queen."

"That's why you chose to follow her, but why do you continue? You have an out. Zathrian would help you. I would help you."

His words felt like a false promise. There was no reason for the Shadow Slinger to help me get out of a binding contract with a demon queen. It made me want to run and never think about him again, but there was a little more work left to do.

"Because I get everything I have ever wanted. I have more gold than nobles in Aloria. Why would I rebel against the queen who gives me everything?"

"Are you satisfied with all that?" Viridian's eyes bore into mine. It was impossible to breathe, to think with him looking at me like that.

I pushed away from him, needing space. "I couldn't be happier if I was a princess." I looked around the room for my clothes.

Viridian appeared behind me. His hands ran over my arms, leaving goosebumps in their wake. "If you could live a different life, what would it be?"

"There's no point in thinking about impossible futures." I was tied to Queen Math'ara until the day I died. I had accepted that life a long time ago.

"Would you want a simple life with a family?"

My chest tightened, hating the questions he asked as his fingers roamed my body. "Even if I wanted that kind of life—which I don't—I can't have children. The queen made sure of that." I grabbed his hands as they ran over my stomach, moving dangerously close to my clit.

Viridian flattened his palm against my body, pulling me flushed against him as if I was his. It was foolish to think that way. The only person I belonged to was the queen.

"You have a choice." His voice was strangely soft in the silent night.

My body shook as I struggled to take the next breath. Viridian didn't understand. He never would. "I don't."

"There is always a choice, even if it feels like an impossible one." His lips brushed against my neck, and it was almost enough to change my mind.

I spun around, placing my hands on his chest. He brushed a strand of hair out of my face as we looked at each other. "We will always be enemies, Viridian. Nothing either of us does will change that. You have your king, and I have my queen."

He pressed his forehead against my head, brushing his nose against mine. "You can change that."

It wouldn't take much to close the space between our lips, but it wasn't fair. My hands shook, and I curled my fingers into fists. "Meet me at the greenhouse tomorrow at noon. I will bring the Aethrium Stone with me. Your king is more deserving of it than my queen. I will give it to you, and then I will leave."

"Queen Math'ara will not be happy with you."

"Nothing I do makes her happy. If taking her punishment means saving this place, then that's what I will do. I've dealt with her punishment plenty of times before."

"Stay."

My heart stopped. "No." I tried to pull away from him, but Viridian grabbed my arm and pulled me back into him.

"Stay," he repeated, and when he kissed me, I didn't fight.

Chapter
21

In crow form, I sat hidden in a thriving fruit tree in the greenhouse. Between the demon king's magic imbued in the walls of the glass building and the touch of magic his human mate had, the greenery was thriving despite the chill that had forced the outside world to go into hibernation. It was impressive, but in a few hours, everything would change. It'd take time, but in weeks or months, the greenhouse would fall to ruin.

It wasn't long before the others began to arrive. Tareen was the first to step into the greenhouse. She looked around, pulling at her fingers. She was early, but she had expected at least one other to be there. Nyri, Aukina, and Reamann walk through the doors next, talking as they made their way over. Elcy fluttered in shortly after, and Satella showed up last, taking her time.

"Reamann shouldn't be here," Elcy said.

"If you think I'm going to let the five of you do this on your own, then you're mad. It's bad enough we're keeping this a secret from Zathrian." Reamann was covered in various weapons, including his favorite sword strapped to his hip.

"Kestria made it clear no one else should be involved." Oh, sweet Elcy. She was trying hard to follow my instructions perfectly.

I had expected the demon guardsman to show up. He and the mermaid were practically glued at the hip. If he tried anything, I was prepared to knock him out, but he wouldn't be able to stop what was about to happen.

"And how do we know we can trust her?" Reamann asked.

"We can trust her," Nyri said. "All Kestria wants is a second chance at life. Isn't that why we are all here?"

It was almost painful to watch. Almost. I had spent my life deceiving those around me. This was a part of the job. A necessary evil.

"I personally don't trust the shapeshifter, but I made a deal with her," Tareen said. "So, what are we doing here, exactly?" The witch looked around. Her cheeks puffed as she pinched her lips together.

"There's more privacy here. At least there should be." Elcy looked at Nyri to confirm.

"I gave everyone the day off," Nyri said. "No one should bother us."

Elcy nodded. "Good."

"Where's Kestria? Shouldn't she be here by now?" Satella asked.

"She said to get started without her. She gave me this diagram." Elcy pulled out a piece of paper with my drawing on it. It was a circle with a flower in the center of it. "She said we need to draw this on the floor, and the rings we have will act as anchors with a pinprick of blood."

There was no need to have them draw on the ground, but the more tasks I gave the residents, the less time they'd have to think about my betrayal. The blood was non-negotiable.

"Blood?" Aukina repeated.

"Are you squeamish?" Satella asked, flashing her teeth.

The mermaid twisted her hair around her fingers. "No. I just thought she needed the rings."

"If she only needed the rings, she wouldn't have bothered asking us for help," Tareen said. "Blood is commonly used in spells, especially old elven ones. The rings will act as a conduit, and our blood will act as a binder between us and the rings. All together, the rings will create a magical barrier to trap the queen inside."

"It's not too late to ask Zathrian for help," Aukina said.

My body tensed. We were too close to the end goal. In a matter of minutes, the Shadow Slinger would show up to retrieve the Aethrium Stone and find himself trapped, allowing me time to go after the king. King Zathrian was in his office. Once I took care of the shadow demon, I would strike the king with my tenisium blades before he realized anything was amiss. It was risky, but with a perfectly timed execution, it'd be easy, and Ethlow would be safe from Queen Math'ara's presence.

As long as they didn't inform the king of my little plan.

"No," Nyri said. "He's busy meeting with a noble from Kinzlea. Besides, we can do this. We are strong, and Kestria will be here any second."

"She's late," Tareen said.

"She'll be here," Elcy assured.

The witch wasn't satisfied with the response, but they got to work. Elcy started to draw the circle, but Tareen quickly took over, telling her she was doing it wrong. They took turns pricking their fingers before touching their blood to the rings.

Everything was set up on their end, which meant it was my turn to take part in the plan. I shifted into a butterfly and moved where they couldn't see me. It was time to shift into a new form, letting horns sprout from my head as I tried on the skin of a demon. I glanced at my reflection in the glass walls. I was the perfect image of Queen Math'ara, except for the clothes. I slid on a ring, and my clothes changed to match the queen. Even those who knew her well would have struggled to tell the difference.

Four more rings went on my fingers. Two to help add to the image of the demon queen, and one to help with unexpected problems. The last one was a gold-banded ring adorned with a purple gem and a drop of my blood: the final piece to the trap

I strode out from behind the trees with the confidence Queen Math'ara held. After years of studying her, I knew her walk, her breath, the slight tilt of her chin. I knew how to embody her perfectly.

"My, my. What is all this?" It was strange to hear the queen's voice come out of my mouth. I knew it wasn't her, but it didn't stop the ice that ran down my spine.

The residents of Ethlow tensed as they took in the demon before them. Reamann was the first to react, pulling out his sword and aiming it at me. I swiped my hand, causing the blade to go flying. To them, it looked like the power of a demon queen, but it was magnetic magic from one of my rings, no more than a simple trick.

Nyri straightened her posture, rolling her shoulders back. She looked like a queen as she faced who she thought was a dangerous demon. She would have been nothing in the face of Queen Math'ara, so she was lucky this was all a facade.

"You are not welcome at Ethlow. Leave now, or Zathrian will have to intervene." Despite the slight shake in her voice, she was brave. Not many had the confidence to stand up to a queen, let alone such a powerful one.

"Not until I have what I'm here for." I made a point to look at each of their faces, planting fear into their minds. "Tell me where my toy is, and I'll think about letting you all live."

"If you're talking about Kestria, she's not your toy. She's a person, one who deserves freedom." Elcy's voice shook as her pixie dust flowed freely. It was almost touching that she was ready to stand up for me.

"She belongs to me, and I won't leave without her. You have two choices. Give her up and live, or die protecting someone you know nothing about." I pressed a button on my second ring, and a ball of electricity floated above my hand. The most it could do was give someone a mild shock. It was nothing more than a show.

The six of them looked around at one another, sharing looks and silently trying to decide what to do. It was inevitable that they would offer me up on a silver platter for my queen to devour. Self preservation made the purest hearts darken.

"She's long gone," Reamann said. "We told her to run far away where you'll never find her." The demon guardsman was lying. For *me*.

"She knows there is no corner of this mortal realm that she can run to. She bears my mark. I will always find her." As long as Queen Math'ara's signet was burned onto my back, I'd never be free.

"Not if we stop you," Nyri said. She grabbed Elcy's hand, which started a chain reaction of all of them holding hands. It was cheesy, and if they were facing the real Math'ara, they'd be dead.

The rings sparked and thrummed as the magic molded together, but it wasn't complete. They didn't know there was a missing piece.

"Why would you risk yourself for someone you don't know?" I crafted my voice to sound disgusted, despite the confusion and curiosity bubbling beneath.

"Because Kestria is our friend," Elcy said.

"I made a deal with her, and I don't go back on my word," Tareen said.

"She saved my life," Aukina said.

"Because she deserves a second chance," Satella said.

"Everyone deserves to be happy and free," Nyri said.

I didn't know how to respond to them. They were foolish and naïve. They didn't understand that none of what they said was true. I wasn't their friend. I was using them. Saving their lives was a manipulation tactic to get them in the palm of my hands. I didn't deserve a second chance. I killed whoever Queen Math'ara asked me to without question and craved violence. My heart had blackened long ago, but they were too nice to see that.

"Because it's not too late." Shadows followed the deep voice. Viridian appeared in front of me, his teal eyes piercing mine. Recognition was clear on his face. He saw past the facade I wore.

Relief flooded the faces of the residents holding hands. They were ready to fight a queen, but they knew they didn't stand a chance. They had been buying time for me to arrive, but they trusted the master of the house to protect them.

"You're wrong." My voice lost the confidence of a queen. "It's decades too late for the shapeshifter."

"I have lived more than my fair share of lives to know that's not true. Align yourself with the correct ally, and you can help shape a brighter future."

"You're a demon of shadows. You know better than anyone that life isn't that simple. Some of us were born with the need to lie and kill. Some of us are crafted into weapons used to destroy the world, even if it destroys us in the process." Anger filled my voice. The Shadow Slinger knew nothing about who I was on the inside. No one did, not even the demon princess I grew up with.

"All it takes is one choice, Kestria." Gasps and murmurs erupted from the others as Viridian said my name.

There was no point in keeping up the farce. I shifted into my human form, shedding the horns and face of the queen. "How did you know?"

"You may be skilled enough to mimic the queen perfectly, but I know your smell. I know your taste." His eyes darkened, reminding me of everything we had done the night prior.

"Thank you for the tip. I'll be sure to mask my scent in the future." I spoke as if his gaze didn't affect me. The moments we shared in the dark of the night no longer mattered. There was nothing Viridian could say or do to make me break from my path. He didn't understand that this was the life I had grown up with, and it was the life I'd die with.

"Enough with the jokes. Be real for once," Viridian said.

I bared my teeth at him as a snarl ripped through my throat. "You don't have the right to judge me. You never let anyone close enough to get to know the real you. You hide in your shadows and terrors, even from the residents you swore to protect."

"Keeping my life private is different than lying to myself. I know who I am. Can you say the same?"

"Fuck you."

"Gladly." His smirk made my core tighten. I hated the demon in front of me. He knew nothing about me. Nothing.

"What the fuck is happening?" Satella whispered to the others.

"You're asking the wrong person," Tareen snapped back.

"I think they like each other," Nyri giggled.

"Stop!" I snapped, unable to bear the chatter.

"All it takes is one choice." Viridian stepped forward, closing the distance between us. "Choose to stay, and you can have a different life."

I couldn't breathe with the shadow demon inches away from me. He was saying all the right things, but they felt wrong. It was wrong to want a life of freedom. It was wrong to betray the queen that gave me everything. But it didn't stop me from wanting a taste of it.

"Stay," Viridian repeated.

The single word broke something in me. I threw my arms around his neck and kissed him deeply, not caring who saw. I pushed him back, unable to stop my hands from roaming. Five more steps. For a moment, I imagined what it was like to live a different life. Four. Eating lunch with those willing to risk their lives for me. Three. Fighting and fucking the shadow demon whenever I wanted. Two. Getting to know the kind demon king. One.

"I'm sorry," I whispered. I slipped the ring with a purple gem on his finger and shoved the shadow demon back. A blast shot from the five rings on the residents, aiming for the ring on the Shadow Slinger's finger. The magic slithered into his veins, making his body freeze. My target fell to his knees, and I hardened my face, refusing to let emotions surface.

The five residents collapsed as exhaustion filled the void left behind from what the rings took from them. They would be okay the next day. Today, it'd feel like they were run over by a bear.

"You lied to us," Nyri said through gritted teeth. Tears mixed with anger in the young human's eyes. She wasn't old enough to know the harshness of the world, but she would know after my lesson left her reeling.

"Of course she lied to you. She's an assassin who works for me."

Chapter
22

I t took everything I had to keep a stone mask on my face in front of the queen. She wasn't supposed to be here. She said she'd give me more time, but she didn't trust me.

The air was thick with her power. It was the type that crawled over my skin and made me sick. Everyone was silent in the presence of the queen. I didn't blame them. For once, their bravery would have been closer to stupidity.

"I'm a little surprised you followed through with the plan." Queen Math'ara strode forward, and I was painfully aware of how close she was. "After you fucked the demon, I thought you were getting soft, but I see now that it was all a ploy to get him to let his guard down."

She knelt in front of Viridian, her eyes piercing his. She wanted to watch his face fall as she rubbed in my betrayal. I wanted to look away, but if she caught me doing that, she'd punish me. Sleeping with the demon was never part of the plan, but it was best everyone thought it was.

"I'm surprised the Shadow Slinger was defeated by a simple shapeshifter. She couldn't even get the image of me right. It was a pathetic attempt at copying me."

My chest tightened. She was right. The copy of her wasn't good enough to deceive Viridian.

Viridian didn't react to the queen. His mask slid into place, a cool calm washing away any emotions he had a moment prior. Maybe for him it was as much of an act as it was for me.

"Leave now, or you will start a war with Kinzlea." Viridian spoke through gritted teeth, fighting the magic pulsing through his body. He wouldn't succeed. The ring sent a mix of liquid iron, tenisium, and magic through his veins, countering his own magic and weakening him every second.

"There's no point, because now that you are incapacitated, my little puppet here is going to kill Zathrian." Queen Math'ara stood, grinning as Viridian snarled. "Oh, she never told you that? I'm not surprised. Nearly everything that comes out of her mouth is a lie. There's a reason I decided to come here myself."

A strangled noise erupted from Nyri, and she looked at me with a face full of betrayal. I wanted to tell her I was sorry, and I would have meant it. It was nothing personal.

"She listens most of the time, but sometimes she tests her leash. In the end, she knows to be a good girl, otherwise she will be punished." Queen Math'ara strode over to me and grabbed my chin. She forced me to look at her, reminding me that I had pushed things too far this time. She wouldn't praise me for capturing the infamous Shadow Slinger or obtaining the Aethrium Stone. Even after I killed Zathrian, she would send me back to Valenmae to endure gruesome punishment for "failing" her.

Nothing I did was ever enough.

"Don't you fucking touch her," Viridian growled.

Queen Math'ara tightened her grip on my jaw, but I bit back the cry of pain. Showing any weakness wasn't tolerated.

The queen glanced over her shoulder, but she didn't let go of me. "You actually care for her, don't you? You knew she was going to betray you, but there was a small part of you that thought maybe she would turn on me if you showed her a little kindness. How pathetically sweet." She grabbed my hair and dragged me over to the Shadow Slinger. She threw me to the ground and stepped on my back. "You underestimated my hold over her. I've been training her for her entire life. If I told her to, she'd thank me for whipping her."

My eyes met Viridian's. He hadn't looked away from me, even as the queen spoke to him. He didn't understand the mistake he made. Even if Queen Math'ara wasn't upset with me, she'd punish me to torture him. I begged him with my eyes to stop, to give up on me. I wasn't worth it.

"If you hurt her, I will kill you." Shadows rolled off Viridian's shoulders, but they faded quickly. His magic couldn't escape my trap any more than he could.

"I'd like to see you try." She crouched down, grabbing my hair. She forced my head back, exposing my neck to her. "The best part is, she likes it, don't you, my pet?"

"Yes, my queen," I said automatically. It was always worse when I didn't give in to her.

Queen Math'ara ran her nail down my cheek, splitting my skin open. Blood dribbled down my face. Viridian jolted, fighting against his restraints, even as they burned him. In a matter of minutes, he'd have the strength of a human.

"Thank you, my queen." The words had been beaten into me over the years.

Queen Math'ara released me. "See. She likes it. You're wasting your energy, Shadow Slinger. She never cared about you. She only cares about her survival. She wouldn't react if I hurt you. She'd celebrate if I killed you. Be grateful I need your services for my new empire."

"There is nothing you could do to make me serve you." Viridian's breath was ragged as his body fought against the poison running through his veins, fueled by the residents he swore to protect.

"Nothing?" Challenge flickered in her face. She grabbed me by the throat, pulling my back against her. Her hand ran down my chest. "What if I offered Kestria as your personal whore? She would make all of your darkest desires come true."

"I'm going to fucking kill you," Viridian snarled. Rage unlike anything I had ever seen burned in his eyes. If he was at full strength, he would have destroyed everything around him, reminding the queen exactly who he was.

My body hit the ground as Queen Math'ara lifted her hand, sending a bolt of electricity into Viridian. His body seized, and dark purple blood dripped down his nose. He didn't have the strength to withstand her attack.

I couldn't stand the sight.

I couldn't stand the queen.

I was the only one who was allowed to hurt Viridian. If he bled, I wanted it to be from *my* knife.

I was going mad.

I had spent too much time at Ethlow. It was the only explanation.

I forced back my thoughts, refusing to react.

"See?" Queen Math'ara dropped her hand. "Not even a blink of care, unlike those around you with tears in their eyes."

Nyri had streams flowing down her face. She felt stupid for helping me and worse for keeping this all a secret. Elcy also had tears staining her cheeks. She had believed in me, believed I was good, and I proved her wrong. Satella looked horrified. She wanted to give me a second chance, like the one she had gotten, but she had learned that not everyone was deserving of atonement. Aukina was too stunned to cry, but her tears would come later. Tareen was livid. I broke her trust, something that was not easily repaired.

The five of them agreed to help me escape from my queen, and I stabbed them in the back.

"One choice," Viridian said, looking me in the eyes.

Only if it was that easy.

Queen Math'ara shocked him again, and I felt sick.

"Stop," I whispered. The moment the word escaped, I knew I messed up.

The queen stopped, slowly turning her attention to me, as if she couldn't believe I had spoken either. Her perfectly crafted assassin had the audacity to speak back to her. She had always seen me as a failure, even if I fulfilled her tasks. It was about time I lived up to her expectations.

"Excuse me?"

I had two choices: grovel or take a stand. One option ensured death. One ensured punishment.

I didn't have words.

"Get up," Queen Math'ara growled.

I stood as ordered. I couldn't defy the queen. It wasn't only my life she'd take. She'd kill everyone in the room with the exception of Viridian, who she would use to do her evil deeds.

"Did you tell me to stop?" She lifted her perfectly shaped brows, her eyes flaring. The quieter she was, the angrier she was.

"We're wasting time. If we want to succeed with killing the king, we need to move now. *I* need to move now." My choice was made. Act as if I hadn't been defying her, a secret third option.

The queen studied me carefully, searching for the lies on my tongue. She wouldn't find any. I was ready to move on, finish the job, and go home. Staying had never been an option, and it never would be.

"Do you think I'm mindless?"

"No, I—" Her hand hit my face with a force that threw me off balance.

"You know better than to speak." A jolt of lightning hit my body, making it impossible to breathe.

I stumbled backwards, clutching my chest. My heart stopped for a second, and the pain radiated through my nerves. Another shock hit my body, and I fell to my knees. She wouldn't kill me, but she wasn't afraid to bring me to the brink of death. She could kill Zathrian herself without his right-hand demon in the way. She didn't need me.

I looked around at the horror-stricken faces. I might have betrayed them, but I didn't lie about everything. I was a prisoner in my own life. Nyri sobbed as she watched me. Satella's eyes were wide and glistening. Tareen's face was tight. Elcy looked nauseous. Aukina wasn't looking at me. She was looking behind the queen at Reamann, who held his sword, ready to strike.

No.

I tried to mouth the words, but my body wouldn't work. The lesser demon didn't understand the mistake he was about to make. I moved to stop him, but another jolt hit my chest, freezing me in place. She wasn't going to stop until I passed out. To punish me. To punish Viridian. To prove she was the most powerful demon in the room.

My fingers dug into the dirt, fighting against the unconsciousness looming on the horizon. I looked at Viridian, ready for his disappointment to meet my gaze. I betrayed him, tricked him, stabbed him, and refused to listen to him. If anyone had done one of those things to me, I would have left them behind and never looked back.

But there was no hatred in his eyes. He looked at me as if it wasn't too late, as if I could choose a different life.

Maybe he was right.

I forced myself to sit up, pushing through the pain. I had been through worse at the hands of the queen. I met her eyes, my jaw hard. My hands shook, my nerves fried from the queen's lightning magic.

"What's wrong with you?" she snarled. Her composure fractured as she realized she was losing control. She lifted her hand to shock me, but a blade pierced her chest.

Reamann twisted his sword. "You will not harm my king. You will not harm Kestria."

Queen Math'ara spun on the demon guard. A blade to the chest was nothing for the demon queen, and Reamann knew that. He wasn't trying to kill her. He was buying me time, because for whatever reason, he believed in me. He was stupid and foolish. He was a bright light in a world filled with darkness, and I understood why Aukina loved him so deeply.

I pushed to my feet, refusing to give in to the pain. I reached for the tenisium dagger at my thigh, but it was too late.

Queen Math'ara pulled the blade from her chest and spun it around. She aimed for Reamann's heart, and she didn't miss.

Chapter 23

Aukina's scream ripped through the air. She crawled through the dirt, fighting the exhaustion in her body. If she reached Reamann, she'd be as dead as him.

Queen Math'ara grabbed Reamann by the chin and lifted him up. "You stupid little demon. Did you think you could stop me? You are nothing but a bug."

"No, I can't." Reamann looked over the queen's shoulders, meeting my gaze. Despite my betrayal, he risked his life, trusting I would come through and stop all of this.

I closed my eyes and took a deep breath to slow my mind. I didn't have time to think. Only to act. I pulled out the two tenisium blades strapped to my body and pushed past the pain that went all the way to my bones. I had no time to stop. If Queen Math'ara pulled the blade out of Reamann's chest, he'd bleed out with little hope to survive.

I jumped into the air and lunged for the queen. Every second of training and torture she put me through flooded my brain. Every time she threatened my life or others around me. Every time she couldn't bother to thank me for risking my life for her. It all added up to that single moment. I wasn't a person. I was a weapon, silent and swift. I was a dagger, molded and pounded into a deadly blade. I was bent and broken into whatever shape was asked of me.

I did not matter.

I never had.

I was the Infernal Dagger, trained to kill demon rulers.

And that was exactly what I was going to do.

I landed on Math'ara's back, plunging the blade into her shoulder. She shrieked as the tenisium pierced her skin. She threw Reamann to the side and turned on me. She shot a bolt of electricity towards me, but I was already flipping away, easily dodging. She had spent years training me, which meant I knew how she liked to attack, which side she favored, every weakness of hers.

"Stop this now," Queen Math'ara said with an icy tone—the one used on me when I was a wild child. I had quickly learned that tone meant months in a dungeon, but not this time.

"No." The word sounded strange to me.

"Excuse me?"

"No." I spoke louder, straightening my back and spinning my dagger in my palm. The queen's blood dripped down the black blade. She wasn't invincible. Today would end in one of two ways: either with my death or with hers. I refused any other option, not with the cries of a mermaid piercing my ears as she continued crawling towards her lover.

"You've grown weak, Kestria."

"No." I shook my head. "I've never been weak. If I was, you would have picked someone else to do your dirty work. You've said it yourself. You only accept the best, and that's exactly what I am.

I am the best assassin in the mortal realm, but I'm done. With this life. With you."

"You forget you belong to me." Queen Math'ara squeezed her hand and the mark on my back burned.

A scream escaped my mouth, and I collapsed to my knees. If she didn't stop, I'd lose consciousness, but I was too skilled for that. She had made sure pain wasn't enough to stop me from completing her tasks.

Viridian roared, his body shaking as he fought against the trap meant to subdue him. If he had been a lesser demon, he would have collapsed with exhaustion minutes ago. He was conscious because of his strength, but he'd never break free. I was on my own as I faced the queen.

I forced myself to my feet. Pain was nothing but a motivator. I chucked a tenisium dagger, and it embedded itself into the queen's hand. The active burning on the signet stopped, but a residual pain pulsed in waves, reminding me of every time she made me suffer to teach me a lesson.

My breath was heavy as my body struggled through the aches and pains, but my mind was clear.

"You thought if you could keep me under your foot, you could control me forever. If you shoved me into the mud enough times, you thought I would grovel and try harder for approval." I palmed the last tenisium dagger I had. This one wasn't going to leave my hand until the queen took her last breath.

"You're talking too much, Kestria," the queen growled.

My throat tightened instinctively. With the queen, I wasn't meant to be seen nor heard. Assassins were supposed to be nothing more than shadows.

"I know, but I think I like talking. Everyone is always talking here. Talking about who is sleeping with who. Talking about the food, the weather, the latest drama. Talking about everything and nothing, and it's fascinating. These people are fascinating." There was a 15 percent chance I'd distract the queen enough by talking in order to make a perfectly timed strike. There was a 70 percent chance I'd irritate her enough to attack again, but she was the image of collected emotions. When she attacked, it'd be calculated and precise. She would go for my jugular to prove her point.

"Enough," Queen Math'ara snapped, and I couldn't stop my visceral reaction.

She ripped the dagger from her hand and dropped it. She didn't need physical weapons to destroy her enemies. She held contracts with nearly every citizen of Aloria, the capital of Valenmae. The more contracts a demon held, the more powerful they were, and Queen Math'ara captured every one possible. She wanted to be the strongest demon ruler.

She lifted her hand to attack, but at the last second, she switched directions, aiming at Aukina, who was trying to reach her lover. I shouldn't have cared about her or the demon guardsman bleeding out a few feet away from her, but a single hit from the queen would destroy the mermaid and the demon guardsman.

There was an impossible time to react, but I was capable of the impossible. Queen Math'ara made sure of that. I slid in front of

Aukina and Reamann, lifting my black dagger in time to block the queen's attack. The electricity bounced off the tenisium and hit a glass panel, causing it to shatter. The queen didn't waste time attacking again, this time aiming for Satella.

Astoria's grief would have been astronomical if the only one who captured her heart in a millennium died. I refused to let that happen.

I was faster than the queen, sliding in front of the vampire before the bolt of magic left the demon queen's hand. It was easy to read her body language and predict where she was going to move before she did. Every time she had used her powers on me, I had been studying her. I knew the queen better than anyone else.

I angled the blade with calculated precision, and the attack bounced off and hit Queen Math'ara in the chest. She stumbled back, and I was already moving. I sprung onto her, scratching her face with the claws of a bear. I stabbed the dagger through her uninjured wrist, pinning her hand to the ground. She tried to pull away, but the black metal drained her strength. Her skin tore as she fought to get free, but she couldn't fight against the tenisium.

I stabbed an iron dagger through her other hand to stop her from struggling beneath me. That one wouldn't last, but it'd make her bleed.

"Stop this nonsense," Queen Math'ara snarled. She was losing her composure. She was scared.

I grabbed another dagger and held it to her neck. If I slit her throat, it wouldn't have been enough to kill her. Killing a strong demon was unheard of. Because of that, the five demon rulers were left unchecked with their power.

"Kestria, you're not good enough. Kestria, you should've done better. Kestria, you're weak." Her words from decades of scolding burned in my head and in my throat. "Tell me one more time what you think of me." I bared the fangs of a snake at her, wishing they were filled with the venom in my heart.

"You'll never be worth anything," Queen Math'ara said. "You're destined to be alone. Even if you kill me and gain your precious freedom, do you think these people will accept you after you betrayed them? You could return to Myst'elle, but once she learns you killed her mother, she'll turn her back on you. You will have nothing and no one and will disappear without me."

I stabbed my dagger through her neck, cutting her vocal chords. It'd stop her from speaking temporarily until her increased healing repaired the damage.

"You're probably right, but I'd rather be alone than live another day tied to you."

"Kestria!" Viridian growled in warning, but he was too late.

Queen Math'ara grabbed my neck and blasted her magic directly into my throat. She had freed her hand from the regular dagger while distracting me with her words. The jolt burned my throat, making tears stream down my face. If that had been a full power attack, it would have killed me instantly, but the tenisium had drained enough of her power that it made it less deadly.

I had seconds before it killed me, and there was no one to save me.

Reamann was bleeding out only a few yards away.

The other residents couldn't stop a queen without risking their own lives.

Viridian was stuck in the trap I set for him.

There was only one who could save me.

I reached towards the tenisium dagger discarded by the queen, but it was too far away. I pressed the ring with an opal on it, and the dagger appeared in my hand. I ripped the second black dagger from the queen's wrist, fighting through the unconsciousness that lingered at the edges of my vision. With all the strength left in my body, I swiped my hands in an X motion.

Queen Math'ara's eyes widened briefly as she realized it was over, but then her body slumped as her head rolled away. Dark purple blood dripped down my face, mixing with my own red blood, and I fought past the exhaustion that went deep into my bones.

My back erupted into flames, and my body seized as pain rippled through the signet on my spine. Power seeped from my skin, and it felt like a piece of me disappeared. I gasped for air, but my lungs didn't want to work. I was going to die with the queen. It was only fitting. The things I had done were not things I could come back from.

Then it was gone all at once. A weight lifted off my body, and breathing came easier. An emptiness settled into my bones, but the pain from the mark was gone. Despite not being able to see it, I knew the queen's mark was no longer on my body.

Silence took over the greenhouse for several seconds before the mermaid's cries replaced all sound.

"Reamann!" Aukina screamed, crawling the last few feet to him. The fear in her voice was a fear I had never felt before. I had never let myself get close enough to anyone to tremble in their death.

The sword had been ripped from his chest when Queen Math'ara discarded him to focus on me. Blood soaked his shirt, too much for anyone to survive. It'd take a miracle to save him, but miracles didn't exist.

"Satella!" Aukina's voice cracked, barely making the name audible, but the vampire was already in action.

"The Bleeding Heart Lily potion," Nyri said.

"We don't have time to get it," Satella said. Her hands pressed against Reamann's chest in a futile attempt to stop the bleeding. "Don't you fucking die on me, you idiot."

I moved towards Viridian, knowing if anyone could help, it was him. I pulled the ring off his finger, and his body slumped with freedom.

"Save him," I whispered.

Viridian disappeared in a burst of shadows. It shouldn't have been possible. The ring should have zapped all magic from his body in the time it was wrapped around his finger, but the Shadow Slinger was no normal demon. Some said he was stronger than all other demon rulers.

"You have to save him." Aukina sobbed, tears streaming down her face.

"We're going to do everything we can." Elcy grabbed the mermaid's hand and held her close. They were all exhausted, barely able to move after the rings took more than they bargained for.

I stared as the scene unfolded, no one looking at Queen Math'ara's body or myself. I couldn't move, not that I could've done anything to help. I didn't have any healing tonics to heal that kind of wound.

"The purple flowers," Nyri said.

"They won't work," Tareen said. "For them to heal, they have to be processed."

"We have to try." Nyri ripped multiple flowers from their stems and brought them over.

"Crush one and put it in his mouth," Satella ordered. Nyri did as the vampire said while Satella shoved the other petals into the wound.

It was futile. Blood pooled around the half-demon. Maybe he would stand a chance if he was in his demon form, but he was weaker as a human.

Shadows erupted, and Viridian held a bottle in his hand. Satella snatched it from him and poured it down Reamann's throat. "Come on, you fucker. Not like this."

Reamann's chest moved slower, as if his body was giving up.

Astoria appeared, a bright smile on her face. The moment she saw everything happening, her smile dropped. She looked at me, and her eyes started glistening. "What happened?" She was speaking to me.

"Queen Math'ara." My voice croaked, even with a whisper. My throat was burned from the demon queen's magic.

The grim reaper looked at the demon queen, and her eyes widened as she put the pieces together. "You killed her."

I didn't respond. I couldn't as the mermaid's sob pierced my ears.

"Don't leave me. Please don't leave me."

"The potion will work, right?" Nyri asked Satella.

"I don't know." Satella kept pressure on the demon's wounds, but there was blood everywhere.

"It saved me. It has to save him." Tears streamed down Nyri's face.

"You were poisoned," Tareen said. "And he's lost a lot of blood. It's two completely different situations."

The grim reaper walked over to me, her eyes focused on the headless queen. "A queen is dead."

"And a new one will rise in her place." My voice was raw, making it crack as I spoke.

With a swipe of her hand, her scythe appeared. She lowered her blade to the queen's chest. The moment the metal touched the lifeless body, it ripped a black puff of smoke from the queen's chest. The scythe guided the soul of the demon to a small charm the reaper had on her belt. No one noticed the reaping of the queen's soul as Reamann sat on his deathbed.

"He's not going to make it, is he?" I asked.

Astoria didn't respond, but the tick in her jaw said enough. She was here to reap two souls.

Aukina cupped Reamann's face. "I love you, Reamann. Do you hear me? I love you. You can't leave me. You were my second chance."

"I love you, Aukina," Reamann barely managed to say.

Aukina pressed his hand against her face. "Fight for me. Please. You can't die."

Reamann didn't respond. He never would.

"No!" Aukina screamed. "Take me. Don't take him. Please."

"It doesn't work that way." Astoria's voice was soft, but tears streamed down her face. I had seen her reap plenty of souls, and she never cried over them. She stopped next to Reamann's body.

I pushed to my feet as the demon stopped moving. I didn't belong here. I never would. I didn't deserve to witness this moment, but I couldn't bring myself to move.

Aukina blocked the reaper's way. "Please."

"I promise I'll take good care of him." Astoria wrapped her arms around the mermaid, and the simple gesture broke her. Sobs wracked Aukina's body, and she couldn't breathe. She'd never be okay after losing the love of her life.

The reaper passed Aukina into Nyri's arms before pulling out her scythe for a second time. When the tip touched the demon, a silver ball emerged from his chest, shining brightly. Aukina tried to reach for it, but Nyri and Elcy held her back.

"Please don't take him. I'll do anything."

Astoria's eyes glistened. "I have to get him to the underworld. I'm sorry." The reaper stepped back, disappearing with Reamann's soul. A scream that could shatter hearts erupted from the mermaid, and she collapsed to her knees. Tears filled the eyes of everyone in the room except two.

I turned and walked away from the mess I created. The last thing they needed was for a lonely assassin to get in their way.

Chapter 24

Everyone gathered in the courtyard outside Ethlow to mourn the passing of the demon guardsman. Reamann was loved by everyone. He had helped out anyone who needed it, but there was a small group that was particularly quiet.

I sat on the roof, watching as the estate grieved. I had no right to join them, but I couldn't bring myself to go. Soon. I would leave them to pick up the pieces I broke in peace.

Jasper nuzzled my side, trying to comfort me, but I didn't deserve it. I pet him mindlessly, trying to reassure him I was okay, but I wasn't sure I was. I grew up surrounded by death, and then I was the one who spread it. I had killed 235 beings in my lifetime. 236 if I counted Reamann, but he didn't die by my hand, so I hadn't decided if he was part of that tally.

Jasper settled next to me, tucking his wings in as he rested his head on my lap.

I felt numb, making it hard to react as shadows crawled towards me.

I closed my eyes and breathed in the scent of leather. Maybe for the last time.

I waited for the Shadow Slinger's retaliation. If he decided to plunge a dagger through my heart, I wasn't going to fight him. There was only a five percent chance of that happening, but part of me wished it was higher.

Viridian sat next to me. His fingers brushed against mine, but he didn't say anything. My heart squeezed, reminding me of the ache in my body. My rapid healing abilities allowed me to move, but it'd be days before I fully recovered from the queen's attack.

Zathrian stood at the front of the crowd, dressed in black formal wear. He took a steadying breath to hide his emotions, but it was written all over his face. He felt like he had failed to protect Reamann, but there was nothing he could have done. Despite that, the death of the demon guardsman would haunt him and the estate for years.

"Yesterday, we lost one of our brightest residents. I have no words to express the pain we feel, but we will honor him for protecting this estate." The king continued on, but I struggled to pay attention.

"Does Zathrian know what happened?" I asked.

"He knows the important pieces."

"Does he know I killed Queen Math'ara?"

"He knows she died. He knows she was here to kill him."

I tapped my fingers against Jasper's head. "Why keep me out of the story?"

Viridian took my hand in his. "Because if he knew the truth, he'd be obligated to report you to the council, and they would call for your death. They wouldn't care that you killed her to protect others or that she was here to kill the sire and start a war."

"You don't want me dead for lying?"

Viridian didn't respond. He didn't have to. I already knew the answer. If he wanted me dead, I would have been.

"You're leaving." His tone held no question, but the air was thick with the unknown.

"I can't stay. They'll never forgive me for the guardsman's death." I knew better than to expect the shadow demon to tell me it wasn't my fault. It wasn't my blade that pierced his heart, but it was my choices that put him in the dangerous position.

"Nyri asked me to tell you thank you."

I blinked once, twice, trying to figure out if I was hallucinating. I huffed a laugh, shaking my head. "She is too good for this world."

"Good comes in different forms."

A small part of me wanted to believe he meant me, but it was impossible. We knew who we were, and we weren't the self sacrificing type. I didn't kill the queen to protect the others. I snapped, unable to take her pressure for a second longer.

"I will never be the good this world needs."

Viridian squeezed my hand, and I squeezed it back. We both knew how the other felt. We didn't need to say it out loud, so we sat in silence, taking in the last few minutes we had to just be ourselves.

"I could have helped you fight the queen. I wouldn't have let her touch you."

"I know." Looking back, I knew if I had taken Viridian's offer of help before the queen arrived, the demon guardsman would have been alive, but turning on Math'ara had never been in the plan. "I didn't need someone to protect me. I had to be the one to free myself."

There was so much more I wanted to say, but I never would.

"Don't go."

I looked at Viridian for the first time. His eyes were already focused on me, and my heart jumped. In a perfect world, I'd stay with the Shadow Slinger and work to earn the forgiveness of the residents I betrayed. Zathrian would welcome me with open arms, because that was the type of demon he was. I'd build a new life, one where others cared about me and where I opened my heart to them, to Viridian.

But that was never the life I was designed to live.

I reached into my pocket and pulled out the Aethrium Stone. I held it out for Viridian to take. "Here. For your king."

Viridian hesitated. "You've changed."

"People don't change. Not really." I took his hand and pressed it into his palm.

Viridian wrapped his fingers around mine, the ancient artifact separating us. "Stay."

It was a command, a plea, a useless hope.

"I have to go back to Valenmae. Princess Myst'elle will become queen, and she has a good heart, like your king. She's going to need someone to protect her. Someone to do the dirty work."

"We will always be enemies, and nothing will change that." He repeated my own words back to me. "You knew. Even if you chose freedom, you were never going to stay." Viridian took the Aethrium Stone and slid it into his pocket.

I shrugged. "I've thought about it."

"You knew."

There had never been a choice to stay. I was loyal to Queen Math'ara by force, but I was loyal to Princess Myst'elle by choice.

"Myst'elle was my first friend. She found me on the street when I was only five, and we spent the day running through the grass and talking to dragonflies. She didn't care who I was, but she grabbed my hand and pulled me along with her. Even when things were hard, she had this way of smiling at me that made me feel seen." Queen Math'ara always hated our friendship, but she hadn't been able to keep Myst'elle away from me. Without her, I might have become a monster like the queen.

"She is lucky to have you."

"And Zathrian is lucky to have you. Every bright light needs a shadow to follow it." I huffed a laugh at the irony. The Shadow Slinger and the Infernal Dagger were the same coin, just a different side.

Snow began to fall from the sky. I held out my hand and let a snowflake hit it. It melted against my skin, but as a flurry of powder continued to rain down, it stuck to everything.

"Ethlow's first snow of winter," I noted. "That's my sign to leave." I stood, brushing a bit of snow from Jasper's nose. The wyvern was built for cold weather, but it didn't stop me from worrying about him.

"You don't believe in signs." Viridian's shadows formed a shield above Jasper's head.

A snarky reply sat on the tip of my tongue, but it wasn't fitting for the moment. I settled for the truth. "I don't like snow."

"Is that the real reason you wish to return to Valenmae, the ocean city?" Viridian quirked an eyebrow. He ran his hand over Jasper, and my wyvern chuffed in response.

"I hate the ocean, too."

"If you could live anywhere, where would you go?"

I hadn't thought about that question before. It had been futile while under Math'ara's thumb. "There's no point in thinking about what ifs."

Viridian ran his hand down my spine before grabbing my hips and turning me to face him. "There is no point in asking you to stay." He studied my face, searching for the answer to the question he hadn't asked. He'd find the knowledge he wanted. If he asked me again with his hands on my body, I'd consider never returning to Valenmae.

He didn't ask.

I didn't want him to.

The demon brushed my cheek, wiping the fallen snow that wetted my skin. I didn't cry, so there was only one explanation for it. "We may always be enemies, Kestria, but no matter where you are, no matter which side we fight for, you will always be mine."

His hand slid through my hair before pulling my face to his. His lips were warm against the cold air. Our lips moved together slowly, savoring the moment of our last kiss. His breath was a whisper of what could have been but never would be. Viridian saw my flaws, experienced my blood lust first hand, yet he saw me. He protected me. He asked me to stay. There had never been one to see me the way he did, and there was only a .5 percent chance that another would understand me the way the Shadow Slinger did.

I pulled away, unable to say anything as I looked into his teal eyes. In another life, I would have called him mine, but Myst'elle needed me.

I swung my leg over Jasper's back, knowing we had to leave before the snowstorm rolled in.

"This is not the end, Kestria."

"I know." My heart thumped with a feeling I didn't fully understand. "I look forward to stabbing you again, pretty boy."

EPILOGUE

A cool ocean breeze washed over the city of Aloria, but the sun cut through the chill as it reflected off the marble buildings. It was strange to be back in the city of fae no longer ruled by Queen Math'ara. It was quiet in the early morning hours. No one had heard the news about the queen's death. Few would before the royal court. Would the city rejoice or mourn the loss of their queen?

I landed on the railing on the balcony of the princess's room. Jasper was back in his pen, being pampered by the stable hands. The flight back to Valenmae was spent thinking about what I would tell the princess about her mother. Myst'elle would understand what happened, wouldn't she?

The queen's last words rang in my head. If Myst'elle knew the truth, she'd hate me. While Math'ara had been unkind to most and laid out harsh rulings for her people, she doted on her daughter. Myst'elle didn't see the horrors I did. She didn't experience them.

I shifted into human form, but I hesitated. There was one thing I could offer her that would stop her from sending me away. I reached into my pocket and pulled out the Aethrium Stone. Any day now, the object I gave to Viridian would revert back into a ring, and my final betrayal would come to fruition. It would make the separation easier, knowing he hated me for jilting his king.

Maybe Zathrian could have used the artifact to save his kingdom and then the rest of the mortal realm, but Myst'elle was young. She was to become queen and join the ranks with demons that were a millennium old. She needed every edge she could get.

Not to mention, it gave the Shadow Slinger a reason to come after me. A reason to cross paths again.

The pad of my finger brushed against the empty space on my finger that had held the thin black ring for years. It was unnerving to not be able to see a second into the future at all times, and my hand felt naked from the missing ring. It had been gone for days, and I knew the exact moment it had disappeared.

It was an excuse to go on a hunt.

The Shadow Slinger and I were the same coin, only different sides.

My smirk faded, knowing I couldn't hold off any longer. It was time to approach my childhood friend and give her the news of her mother's death. I unlocked the door and slipped inside. Arajin stood in front of the princess, her face grim. Silver piercings covered her dark, pointed ears. Mixed with her tight leather corset, the court advisor looked killer. Only those that knew the ancient being knew she was one of the most loving demons in all of Valenmae.

Myst'elle's eyes glistened, and her hands shook. "Are you sure?"

Arajin grabbed the princess's arms. "Word just came from King Zathrian." Word about the queen's death.

"What happened?" Myst'elle's lip wobbled, but she held her chin high as she was taught to do.

"Her death occurred under unknown circumstances, but they are looking into it, according to the message passed via shadows." Arajin's face held firm, hiding any emotions. She had been Math'ara's advisor since the Great Demon Wars.

"Demons lie." Myst'elle wrapped her arms around herself, digging her nails into her skin.

"We will investigate the truth, and we will punish those responsible," Arajin said.

I couldn't tell them what really happened. They would never understand. I fingered the Aethrium Stone in my pocket. Later. I'd give it to her later.

"I don't know what to do." Myst'elle struggled to keep her composure. She was only thirty years old, a babe compared to the queen. The princess hadn't lived long enough to learn to keep her composure, and the queen coddled her. She had gone through the basic training, but it was nothing compared to what I had lived through. Math'ara had thought herself invincible. She expected to live forever, which meant Myst'elle would have never ascended to the throne. She didn't need to be strong.

Math'ara was wrong.

"You become queen and take over protecting this kingdom," Arajin said. "Just like your mother wanted you to." The advisor was lying. She knew better than anyone that Myst'elle was never supposed to be queen, but Arajin loved the princess like her own.

She was the one who read the princess bedtime stories when the queen had been too busy.

"I don't know if I can do that."

I tapped the dresser, bringing attention to myself. Arajin's face tightened as she noticed me. She didn't know the truth. There were only a handful of people who did, and not even the king was aware of what happened.

"You can do anything," I said, looking at Myst'elle. "And you'll have a team behind you."

The moment the princess saw me, she rushed over, throwing her arms around me. "Kestria! Did you hear?"

I tapped into my training, hiding my emotions with ease. "I knew the moment it happened. Her mark on my back is gone, and I returned as soon as possible." Myst'elle was to become queen, and she needed me. She needed as much support as possible. If she learned I was the one to kill her mother, she'd never speak to me again. For her sake, I couldn't let that happen.

"I don't understand. She was the strongest woman I knew. I didn't think it was possible for anyone to kill her."

I patted the princess's back, unsure of how to comfort her.

Arajin strode forward, peeling the princess off me and wrapping her into her chest. "No one is invincible. Even the strongest can be taken down." She stroked Myst'elle's hair. It was the same color as the queen's. She also inherited the queen's height, eyes, and horns. Despite the similarities, no one said the princess was the spitting image of the queen. Myst'elle didn't have the same sharpness to her features, and she didn't have a darkness weighing her down.

Myst'elle pulled back from Arajin, straightening her spine. Her face hardened as reality set in. "My mother wouldn't want me to cry over her. I'm going to be queen soon. I have to be strong."

My heart ached for the princess, but I didn't regret my decisions. Valenmae was better off without Math'ara. Myst'elle would rule with compassion, and I would be there to ensure no one tried to hurt her. If they did, I'd be waiting in the shadows with my blades, ready to tear them apart.

I sat on the roof of the palace, watching the sunset fall over the ocean. I chucked pieces of bread on the roof tiles and watched as pigeons gathered. It was comforting to have the birds around me. They were predictable, and they told me about the whispers of the city when they liked me.

"I see you like to cause mayhem wherever you are."

I jumped to my feet, pulling out two daggers as I turned to face the shadow demon. "You have some audacity showing up in my city."

Viridian looked at my weapons and smirked. "Do you plan on stabbing me?"

"I'm thinking about it."

The demon huffed a laugh, his eyes twinkling. "You'd have to catch me first."

"Is that a challenge?" I spun my daggers in my hand, debating about throwing one. He'd see it coming and knock the blade away, but it'd rile him up.

"Is it a challenge if I know I'll win?" His cocky smirk made me want to drive my knife into his side.

"I should kill you for walking on enemy territory." My breath quickened as excitement rushed through my veins. "And for stealing my personal property."

"And I should kill you for stealing the Aethrium stone." His bat-winged horns fluttered as his lips tugged into a smirk.

"I dare you." I flashed a mouth full of sharp teeth at him.

Viridian chucked a dagger at me, but I moved before it left his hand. I rushed at the demon head on. His shadows wrapped around my wrists, but I was already dropping my daggers. Viridian grabbed the back of my head, pulling me into a kiss. I should've demanded an explanation as to why he was in Valenmae or told him to leave, but for a moment, I let my guard down, unable to resist his touch. I would never admit it out loud, but Viridian was mine as much as I was his. There might come a time when we were on opposite sides of the battlefield, but until then, I'd steal whatever time I had with him in the shadows.

WANT MORE?

Want to see more of these characters? Check out ***The Demon Queen's Rise,*** Princess Myst'elle's journey to becoming the demon queen of Valenmae. The demon princess is determined to live up to her mother's reputation and become the best queen she can, but when secrets start to unfold, Myst'elle discovers her mother wasn't the queen she thought she was. As cracks form beneath the palace of Valenmae, Myst'elle must fight to protect her kingdom from attacks from the underworld all while dealing with a demon thief who is skilled at stealing hearts. Will she be able to rise to be the demon queen her kingdom needs, or will the pressures of royalty make her crack?

Coming Early 2025

Author's Note

T hank you so much for taking time to read my book! If you've made it this far, I would greatly appreciate it if you took the time to leave a review on Amazon/Goodreads. As an indie author, reviews are essential for gaining more visibility. All reviews are appreciated! If you ever have any questions, concerns, or general comments, please feel free to reach out to me directly at evereri.theauthor@gmail.com!

ALSO BY EVERERI

Read more in The Demons of Kinzlea

The Demon King's Pet
The Demon King's Cook
The Demon King's Healer
The Demon King's Librarian
The Demon King's Teacher
The Demon King's Assassin

Coming Soon!

The Demon Queen's Rise
Coming in early 2025

The Unfortunate Fate of Mates

Available on the Dreame App:

The Four Beta Brothers
The Stolen Wolf Princess
The Long Lost Luna
The Unwanted Wolf
The Blood Moon Twins

ACKNOWLEDGEMENTS

I can't believe this is the last book in the Demons of Kinzlea. At the beginning of 2024, I decided to take one of the biggest risks of my life and lean into being an indie author. I have been a serialized fiction writer for many years, but diving into the indie author world was different from what I had been doing. It has been terrifying and rewarding all at once. I have a long way to go on my journey to get where I want to be, but I wouldn't be where I am without so many amazing people in my life.

Kelly, I can't thank you enough for being my alpha reader. You have given me so many ideas that has only made these books and my writing better. Thank you for taking the time to help me edit this book specifically. I fully believe this is the best book I have written quality and characterization wise, and it is heavily thanks to you. I will be forever grateful for your help in this process and constant support.

Paula, you continue to believe in me when so many people doubt my choices. Thank you for always supporting me in my wild dreams and for reading my books. You are the best sister I could ask for, and I appreciate everything you've done for me.

Amanda, thank you for all the times spent brainstorming with me. You helped me take my ideas from the clouds and build it into something concrete. Talking about my world with you is so much fun, and your love for a certain male character has been very inspiring!

Lauren, you are a bright light in my world, and I'm extremely lucky to have you in my life. Knowing you love this series has inspired me to keep pushing forward. Thank you for always listening to my doubts about this journey. There are days I question if I on the right track, but you never doubt it. For that, I will be ever grateful.

Michelle, I can't believe you've been reading my writing since I was fifteen. Your support means the world to me, and when you get invested in my characters and storylines, it inspires me to keep writing and improving. I can't wait to share my future books with you!

Sam, thank you for always being there to give me name suggestions (I'm sorry Lonis wasn't up to your standards). I love talking to you about my worlds and characters, because you have a way of seeing and understanding the characters in ways that aren't reflected on the page.

To every one of my readers who have fallen in love with this world with me. You inspire me to keep going, even when I have my doubts. I am always working to improve my writing to give you the best story available. Your support means the world to me, and I am forever grateful for that. This is just the beginning of a journey, and I'm excited for every step ahead!

ABOUT THE AUTHOR

 EverEri is a lover of romance, fantasy, and fairytales, and one of her favorite things to do is to bring a story and characters alive through the written word. EverEri began her true writing journey in the paranormal romance world in 2021, and she never plans to turn back. Whether it's demons, dragons, werewolves, merfolk, or other magical beings, she plans to bring her passions to life in each book she writes.

Want to see more?

Follow EverEri on social media:

IG: everlastingeri

Tik Tok: author_evereri

FB: EverEri's Reading Group

Newsletter: evereri.theauthor@gmail.com